"I'll stop if you want me to,"

Denis said raggedly, "but sitting so close to you in the dark is a powerful temptation. Not being able to touch you would be just pure torture."

Oh, God. How could Elizabeth resist him when he talked like that? "For me, too," she admitted. "But what happens later?"

His restless hand moved again, rubbing back and forth on her leg. "We've been in this situation before, sweetheart. Do I have to remind you what happened later?"

A wave of heat made her moan as her memories came flooding back. "No!" It was a cry of frustration rather than a straight answer. "That's not the same. We were engaged then."

"Nothing has changed for me, Elizabeth. You're still my girl, my love. You always have been."

How could she argue when she so badly wanted what he was offering?

Dear Reader,

Whether it's a vacation fling in some far-off land, or falling for the guy next door, there's something irresistible about summer romance. This month, we have an irresistible lineup for you, ranging from sunny to sizzling.

We continue our FABULOUS FATHERS series with *Accidental Dad* by Anne Peters. Gerald Marsden is not interested in being tied down! But once he finds himself the temporary father of a lonely boy, *and* the temporary husband of his lovely landlady, Gerald wonders if he might not actually enjoy a permanent role as "family man."

Marie Ferrarella, one of your favorite authors, brings us a heroine who's determined to settle down—but not with a man who's always rushing off to another archaeological site! However, when Max's latest find shows up *In Her Own Backyard,* Rikki makes some delightful discoveries of her own. . . .

The popular Phyllis Halldorson returns to Silhouette Romance for a special story about reunited lovers who must learn to trust again, in *More Than You Know.* Kasey Michaels brings her bright and humorous style to a story of love at long distance in the enchanting *Marriage in a Suitcase.*

Rounding out July are two stories that simmer with passion and deception—*The Man Behind the Magic* by Kristina Logan and *Almost Innocent* by Kate Bradley.

In the months to come, look for more titles by your favorite authors—including Diana Palmer, Elizabeth August, Suzanne Carey, Carla Cassidy and many, many more!

Happy reading!

Anne Canadeo
Senior Editor

MORE THAN YOU KNOW

Phyllis Halldorson

Silhouette
ROMANCE™
Published by Silhouette Books New York
America's Publisher of Contemporary Romance

For Gerald Halldorson, affectionately known as
Jiggs, who has been my husband, lover and best
friend for a very long time. Happy Anniversary,
darling. The years we've been together have indeed
been golden. If I had them to live over, there's not a
thing I would change.

SILHOUETTE BOOKS
300 East 42nd St., New York, N.Y. 10017

MORE THAN YOU KNOW

Copyright © 1993 by Phyllis Halldorson

ISBN: 0-373-08948-1

First Silhouette Books printing July 1993

Printed in the U.S.A.

PHYLLIS HALLDORSON,

at age sixteen, met her real-life Prince Charming. She married him a year later and they settled down to raise a family. A compulsive reader, Phyllis dreamed of someday finding the time to write stories of her own. That time came when her two youngest children reached adolescence. When she was introduced to romance novels, she knew she had found her long-delayed vocation. After all, how could she write anything else after living all those years with her very own Silhouette hero?

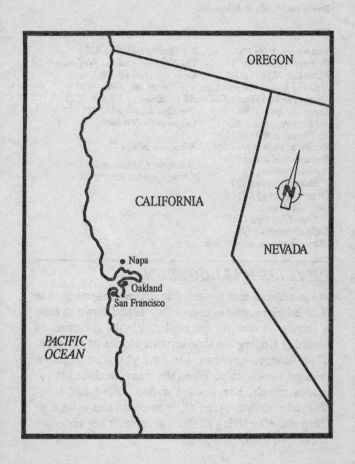

OREGON

CALIFORNIA

NEVADA

Napa

Oakland

San Francisco

PACIFIC
OCEAN

Chapter One

Elizabeth Anne Kelly changed quickly from her green "scrubs" to slacks and a shirt in the nurses' lounge of Sisters of Mercy hospital, then grabbed her purse and hurried from the room. A strong gust of wind rocked her as she stepped out the wide sliding glass doors that opened onto the emergency trauma center. Her unruly red hair was whipped into a frenzy.

The late October day had all the makings of another hot one, and in Oakland, California, that meant humid, sticky and unbearable. The ninety-degree weather they'd been having was highly unusual for the balmy seaside area, and especially for October. So was the dry wind that had come up in the past few hours, blowing around the hot air rather than cooling it.

There was a haunting eeriness in the weather that troubled Elizabeth enough to make her hesitate before continuing on. The air almost seemed to crackle with tension, but that was silly. She was the last person to tune in to static electricity. It must be the heat getting to her.

She had started to move, when a voice from behind called to her. "Hey, Liz, wait up."

She turned to see Pilar Ignacio, her apartment mate and fellow trauma nurse stepping through the automatic door.

"If you're going to the deli down the street for lunch, I'll come along," Pilar said as she grappled with her wind-tossed long, dark hair. "I've been on my feet all morning. I want to just sit back and relax for a few minutes without having to answer a page."

Elizabeth chuckled sympathetically as they headed across the parking lot to the sidewalk. "I know what you mean. Sundays are always a madhouse around here. I'll never understand why people ignore symptoms all week, then decide they have to have treatment on Sunday when all the private doctors are golfing."

Pilar rolled her eyes. "Tell me about it. We had a woman come in this morning from the posh East Bay hills and demand to be seen immediately for a cough she'd had all week."

Elizabeth smiled. "Perhaps I should remind you, friend, that the so-called *posh* East Bay hills is where I was born and raised."

Pilar looked unrepentant. "That's all right, I forgive you for being a poor little rich girl. You've redeemed yourself by becoming an underpaid working peon like me. But that woman had the nerve to insist that she be taken ahead of everyone else because she had a date to play tennis and didn't want to be late."

Elizabeth executed an exaggerated shrug. "What can I say? Obviously you don't understand how exclusive those memberships in the Rolling Hills Racquet Club are," she drawled in her best highbrow tone. "I mean, after all, one can't keep those important people waiting. Besides, who knows what disease one might pick up in our untidy, crowded waiting room."

Both women laughed at their mutual teasing as they approached Mama Rose's Deli and entered. They selected sandwiches and salads at the counter, then picked up glasses of milk and carried their trays to one of the small round tables.

"To get back to your shamefully affluent background," Pilar said. "How come you're sharing a semi-run-down apartment in a working-class neighborhood with me, the daughter of migrant farm workers, when your parents have all those gorgeous empty bedrooms in their mansion up in the hills?"

"Just lucky, I guess," Elizabeth said with a grin, then sobered. "I mean that seriously, Pilar. Life is a lot more meaningful for me down here than it was up there."

She gazed off into space and murmured thoughtfully. "I'm grateful to Deny for making me face what I was becoming, in time to change, even if it did almost kill me."

"Huh?" Pilar had just taken a bite of sandwich and had to swallow it before she could go on. "Who's Deny and what almost killed you?"

Shaken out of her reverie, Elizabeth cursed herself for talking too much. Even after all this time, the subject of Deny was incredibly painful. "Oh, sorry. It's nothing. I was just reminiscing."

"Aw, come on, Liz. You can't keep me hanging like that. I've told you all my grubby little secrets, so how about sharing some of your glitzy ones with me?"

Searing memories that Elizabeth strove to keep tightly in check came rushing back in a cloud of anguish, and she took a deep breath to steady herself. "Glitzy secrets can be just as painful as grubby ones, Pilar," she said slowly. "Denis

O'Halloran was my fiancé. Also my lifelong best friend. He called off the society wedding of the season just a week before it was to take place and left town.''

Pilar set her glass down with a thud. "Oh, my God! Some best friend! Why would he do a thing like that?"

A picture of Deny blurred Elizabeth's vision. Five feet nine inches tall. Fairly short for a man, but he still towered over her five foot two. He had black hair that was always in need of a cut and laughing blue eyes that sparkled with fun. They'd been next-door neighbors, playmates, best friends and sweethearts, until that afternoon in June when he'd shattered all her dreams and left her bereft.

Elizabeth shook her head and the image disappeared. "We...we had a quarrel. Look, I really don't like to discuss..."

Pilar put her hand over Elizabeth's on the table. "Hey, look, I'm sorry, but you did bring it up. Maybe that's a sign that you need to talk about it with someone."

"Yes, Dr. Ignacio," Elizabeth quipped, and withdrew her hand, hoping to get the conversation back onto a lighter plane.

"Go ahead and kid around if it helps," Pilar said, her deep brown eyes filled with compassion, "but we've both had enough psychology classes to know that something that traumatic shouldn't be kept bottled up inside. Did you get counseling?"

"No, my parents suggested it but I couldn't. It was just...just too painful to go over again and again. All I wanted was to get through it and forget."

"But you haven't forgotten, have you?"

Elizabeth swallowed. "No, but I've accepted the fact that Deny was right. We were too young and immature for marriage."

"Then why did he propose to you in the first place?"

Elizabeth shrugged. "Oh, we thought we were in love, and also it was expected of him. From the day I was born, our parents, who were neighbors and best friends, had been planning our wedding. Their fondest dream was to unite the two families and share mutual grandchildren."

"Are you saying that you weren't in love?" Pilar persisted.

Elizabeth squirmed and tried to think of a way to change the subject. "He wasn't, I was. Now can we . . ."

Pilar wasn't about to let go. "When did this happen?"

"Almost three and a half years ago."

"Okay, suppose you just tell me what you quarreled about? Then if you want to drop it, we will, at least for now."

Elizabeth decided to give her friend an abbreviated version and get her off the subject. "Deny'd just graduated from Stanford and was offered a job with a large chemical company in San Francisco. He was going to accept it, but then he got a better offer from a government agency in Washington, D.C., and took it instead.

"I'd finished my sophomore year at San Jose State and was entering the nursing program in the fall. I didn't want to interrupt my education, and I couldn't conceive of moving so far away from home."

Pilar waited, and, when it became obvious that Elizabeth wasn't going to continue, she said, "So?"

Elizabeth took a bite of salad. "So he went to Washington and I stayed home."

Pilar shook her head in exasperation. "I get the impression that you've skipped over a few important details, but I promised not to pry . . ."

Elizabeth couldn't help but chuckle. "Oh, Pilar, for you that's like promising not to breathe, but I'm going to hold you to it for now. I want to enjoy my lunch before we have to get back on the floor."

"Okay, if that's how it has to be," Pilar grumbled, "but don't think I'm going to forget. We'll finish this conversation tonight after dinner."

Ten minutes later they left the deli and stepped out into the hot gusts, but now the sky looked overcast. Again Elizabeth felt the tingle of misgiving. "That's odd. It looks like high fog, but that's not possible in this wind." She sniffed as they walked. "Do you smell smoke?"

Pilar sniffed, too. "Yeah, I do, but where could it be coming from? Surely there's no legal burning around here today."

They hurried on back to the hospital and had no sooner gotten inside the door than the nurse at the admission desk called to them. "Kelly. Ignacio. Where have you been? You're wanted in the auditorium. There's a code-blue alert briefing going on. The whole East Hills section of the city is on fire. We're instituting emergency procedures to handle the casualties!"

Panic exploded inside Elizabeth. "That's where my parents live! I've got to go up there." She turned and ran toward the exit, but Pilar and a uniformed security officer caught up with her just as she reached it.

"Hold on, ma'am," he said. "That area's closed off. They're not letting anyone through."

Elizabeth struggled against Pilar, who was holding her. "Liz, try to calm down. Aren't your mom and dad still vacationing in Greece?"

Elizabeth continued to struggle, impatient to be on her way. "Yes, they are, but Aunt Maggie and Uncle Aidan are up there, and the house... I've got to get things out of the house...."

Pilar shook her. "Hey, wait. I didn't know you had other relatives living there."

"Not really family... Deny's parents...I told you...they live next door to us. I've known them all my life...they're as dear to me as a real aunt and uncle...." Her sentences were coming in gasps as she struggled to break away. "Let me go! I've got to get up there and see if there's anything I can do to help!"

Again the security officer interrupted. "Look, miss, it won't do you any good to try. The whole place is sealed off. All that wooded area is going up like a torch. It happened so fast, and there's a power outage that shut off power to the water pumps. The winds keep shifting and the whole thing's out of control. You can't get through the Caldecott Tunnel—both Highways 24 and 13 are closed and so are all the streets leading into it. The traffic jams are huge and getting worse."

Slowly Elizabeth began to realize that what he said was true, but still the urgent feeling that she had to protect her home and her friends tormented her.

As she stopped fighting, Pilar's grasp loosened. "Honey, if I thought we stood a chance in hell of getting through, I'd drive you up there myself, but we can't do anybody any good if we get stalled in traffic and have to sit in the car all afternoon."

She cleared her throat then continued. "We're needed here, Liz. Pretty soon the casualties will be coming in and we're already shorthanded."

"I know that, but—"

Pilar didn't let her finish. "I can only imagine what you're going through, but don't let your heart rule your head. Stay here and use your training where it will do the most good. Let the ones who know what they're doing evacuate people from their homes."

What Pilar said made sense, and Elizabeth slumped against her. "Yeah. Okay, you're right."

Pilar put her arm around her and led her to a chair. "Do your neighbors have relatives close by who can look after them?"

Elizabeth nodded and sat down. "The last I heard their daughter lived in San Francisco and one son in Berkeley. I don't know if Deny is still in Washington, or where the other two sons are, for sure. Our families haven't been close since the wedding debacle."

"I can imagine," Pilar murmured sympathetically, "but at least you can be sure they have someone looking out for them. As for us, we'd better change back into our scrubs and get up to that meeting so we'll know what's going to be expected of us for the duration of this emergency."

It didn't take them long to find out. By the time the meeting was over, the trauma center had admitted the first of what became a wave of victims. Although the severely burned patients were being taken to the nearby burn center, Sisters of Mercy was getting its share of other medical problems.

A call was put out for all the doctors and nurses who had volunteered for the hospital's disaster team, and soon the place was a mass of activity. Pilar, who had more experience, was assigned to assist the doctors, and Elizabeth was put to work cleaning and bandaging burns and injuries.

She worked methodically, not daring to let her compassion get in the way of her skill as the ambulance crews deposited their patients in the halls and went out again for more. Some of the injured walked in, others were brought in in wheelchairs or on stretchers. All needed attention, and most had to wait for it.

During a short break, she dialed the O'Hallorans' number, but the call didn't go through. The lines were down, and she could only speculate on the fate of them and other life-long neighbors as she returned to her heartbreaking duties.

Elizabeth had managed to shut out the interminable noise and the nauseating smells, but she couldn't ignore the pain, both physical and emotional, that tormented the men, women and children that she ministered to that day.

It was six o'clock, and she'd been on duty for eleven hours, when a male nurse who usually worked in oncology came to relieve her. "Go home and get some sleep," he told her, "because unless they get this fire under control you're sure to be called out again in the middle of the night."

For the first time in hours Elizabeth thought about the fire instead of just the victims of the blaze. "You mean they *still* don't have it controlled?" she asked in amazement.

He shook his head. "Not even close. I came in on the swing shift, and at that time they were battling to keep it from leaping into the evergreen forest above the Claremont Hotel. This one's a real bitch. The eucalyptus trees are actually exploding into flame."

A picture of her stately twelve-room family home nestled among the big old trees on a hillside overlooking the rest of the city and the picturesque San Francisco Bay beyond flashed into her mind. It brought tears to her eyes, but she quickly blinked them back and banished the picture. She'd seen too many people devastated today, she wasn't going to waste tears on the loss of possessions.

As she picked her way down the halls lined with patients on gurneys waiting to be examined, from behind her, a vaguely familiar voice hollered over the din. "Elizabeth, wait."

She turned and looked around for a moment before she saw Deny's father sitting in one of the wheelchairs along the hallway wall. She almost didn't recognize him. His hair was covered with ash, his face darkened with soot. He wore a short hospital gown in place of a shirt, and both hands and arms were bandaged.

She ran back and crouched down beside him. "Uncle Aidan," she gasped as she carefully hugged him. "How did you get here? I've been frantic worrying about you and Aunt Maggie."

Aidan O'Halloran wasn't a big man, but he'd always had the aura of intelligence, wealth and power that more than made up for size. Now, though, he looked exhausted and sick, like all the others being brought in here today. It briefly occurred to Elizabeth that a catastrophe such as this one was a great equalizer. You couldn't distinguish the royalty from the masses, and what's more, nobody cared.

"I didn't know you worked here," he said. "God, but I'm glad I saw you. I'm going crazy and can't get answers from anyone."

Alarm gripped her. "What's happened to you? Are those burns under the bandages? Are you in pain?"

He nodded. "Yes, but they gave me a shot to dull it. It's Maggie I'm worried about. They took us to separate examining rooms when we got here and no one will tell me how she is, or even where she is. Help me, Elizabeth." It was a plea of desperation. "I can't get anyone to listen to me."

"Try to stay calm," she said soothingly. "If she's in this hospital I'll find her, but first I'll need more information. Tell me what happened. Is Maggie burned, too?"

Elizabeth wondered how she could sound so cool and professional when inside she was deeply afraid. *Was Aunt Maggie dead?* She wouldn't be the first one to be brought in today only to die while being treated.

"No," Aidan said, "she's not burned, but you know she has emphysema...." He paused and his shoulders slumped.

"No, I guess you don't know. She developed it after the...after our two families stopped speaking to each other. We didn't even know that you worked here."

She touched his shoulder. "I never blamed you and Maggie for what happened, but Mom and Dad were so upset that..."

"I know," he said without looking at her. "I can't blame them...."

He paused, his expression a study of sadness and regret. "Anyway," he continued, "the fire spread so fast that the air was filled with smoke before we realized how bad it was. Maggie was having trouble breathing. We...we have oxygen at the house.... The fire was away from us...we thought we'd be safe there, but the wind shifted...."

His breath was coming in gasps, and Elizabeth reached out and touched him. "Slow down, Uncle Aidan, and take a deep breath. How did you get out?"

"A rescue team came and took us to safety, but Maggie could hardly breathe. Oh God, I was so afraid I was going to lose her...."

His voice broke on a sob and Elizabeth squeezed his shoulder and fought to keep her own voice steady. "How did you get burned?"

He looked down at his hands and arms. "They look worse than they are," he said almost apologetically. "Just before the helicopter arrived, I noticed a blaze in the ravine behind our property. I grabbed the hose and tried to put it out, but the wind changed direction again and, well, I didn't get out of the way quite fast enough."

A picture of the elderly man engulfed in flames flashed through her mind and made her cringe. "Oh, Uncle Aidan, you could have been killed!"

He turned his bandaged hands over and inspected them. "Yes, well, that's something you think of after the fact."

Elizabeth shuddered. "You were brought here by helicopter?"

He nodded. "Yes."

"Was Maggie conscious when you got here?"

"I'm not sure. They were giving her oxygen...."

"All right," she said soothingly, in spite of her own alarm. "You sit here. I'll go and see what I can find out."

She stood up, but he clutched at her. "Someone will be coming soon to take me to a room. I might not be here when you come back. How will you..."

She patted his shoulder gently. "Don't worry, I'll find you."

It took fifteen minutes of looking into treatment rooms and questioning busy medical personnel before Elizabeth learned that Margaret O'Halloran had been admitted to the hospital with severe respiratory problems and had been taken up to the intensive care unit.

She raced down to the trauma center, where she found Aidan still there and talking to a doctor. "The heavy smoke has put a great strain on her lung capacity," the physician was saying, "and we'll need to monitor her until she can breathe normally again without continuous oxygen."

"May we see her?" Elizabeth asked.

"She's in intensive care, but as soon as the nurses have finished with her you can visit for a few minutes. Don't let her talk or get excited. She needs all her oxygen just to breathe right now."

Upstairs in the ICU waiting room, Aidan fidgeted while they waited. An orderly had come just before they left the trauma center to take him to his room, but he'd insisted on seeing his wife first.

"For heaven's sake, how long can it take to get her settled?" he demanded, his agitation rising with every second. "Maybe something's happened. Go find out, Elizabeth. They'll tell you, you're a nurse."

Her heart went out to the tortured man. He and his wife had been married for over forty years and were seldom separated. "I just did, Uncle Aidan. I told you, she has to be hooked up to several monitoring devices, and they want to clean her up a little. I gather she's as sooty as you are. Try to relax. It won't be much longer."

He continued to fret, and finally Elizabeth went to the nurses' station and found Maggie's chart. There wasn't much information on it yet, but what there was indicated that, barring complications, her condition was uncomfortable but not life-threatening.

She went back to the waiting room to report to Aidan, and the nurse came shortly thereafter to take them to Maggie. Elizabeth had pushed him as far as the open area where the patient cubicles were, then held back. "I'll wheel you to her and then come back and wait here," she told Aidan. "It's probably better if she doesn't see me right now. It's been so long, and things have been so strained between all of us—"

"Don't be silly, girl," he admonished. "You're staying with me. She'll be relieved to know you don't hold a grudge against us, and I need you to tell me how she's really doing. Never did trust doctors to tell the truth."

Elizabeth nodded. "All right. If you're sure—"

Aidan didn't let her finish before impatiently motioning her on.

The intensive care unit was a large area with the monitoring station against one wall, and single-bed, open-ended compartments lined up side by side on the others. All the beds could be seen from the station.

Elizabeth and Aidan were led to one of the cubicles and told not to stay more than five minutes. She wheeled his chair to one side of the bed, then went around to stand on the other side.

Her heart constricted as she gazed at the woman who had been almost as dear to her as her own mother. She looked older and very ill. Her eyes were closed, and she had a bluish-gray pallor that accentuated the lines of fear and exhaustion. She was getting oxygen from a nasal cannula, and there was also an IV in her arm.

Elizabeth waited for Aidan to make the first move. Tenderly he took Maggie's hand and bent over her. "Maggie," he said softly. "It's me. I came as soon as they'd let me."

The woman on the bed opened her eyes and smiled at him. "Aidan." It was little more than a whisper.

"You're going to be all right," he assured her, "but they want to keep you here for a few days."

She looked as if she were going to protest, but he put his finger to her dry lips. "They told us not to let you talk. You need your strength, but I brought you a surprise. Turn your head and look at her."

Slowly Maggie turned, and when her gaze met Elizabeth's, she smiled. "Elizabeth . . ."

A rush of tenderness engulfed Elizabeth, and she leaned down and kissed Maggie's cheek. She couldn't even count the times Deny's mother had fed, bathed and comforted her, and her mother had done the same for Deny. It had been like having two sets of parents until that dreadful day when the friendship between the families had been shattered along with her wedding plans.

"Hi, Aunt Maggie," she said in a voice that quivered with emotion. "I'm a nurse now, and I work in this hospital, so I'll be around to make sure they take good care of you. Don't worry, we'll have you out of here in no time."

Liz saw a tear trickle out of the corner of Maggie's eye just as the nurse came to tell them they'd have to leave.

Elizabeth wheeled Aidan directly to the private room that had been assigned to him on the third floor, and signed him in. The floor nurses welcomed her help in cleaning him up and putting him to bed. After they had him settled and had given him a sedative, the other nurse left and Elizabeth sat down in a chair beside the bed. Now that she could see him without the soot and ash she noticed that he hadn't changed much in the past three years. Even in his mid-sixties, he was still a trim, good-looking man.

"I'll leave in a few minutes and let you sleep," she told him, "but first I need to know if you've been in touch with your family yet?"

He shook his head. "I tried, but by the time we realized we were in danger the phones were out. Rosalie's in the hospital in San Francisco. She had a baby boy yesterday afternoon. Finley's still teaching at Berkeley, but he and his family are out of town this weekend. Seamus lives in Carmel, Glendon in South Lake Tahoe, and, of course, Denis in Washington. There's not much any of them can do, but if they hear about the fire they'll be worried...."

Worried was an understatement, and indicated that Aidan was still not aware of the scope of the disaster. When his family heard about the fire, they'd be terrified. They wouldn't know where their parents were or what had happened to them.

"Congratulations on your new grandson," she said. "I'm sure you don't want Rosey to be upset with worry about you and Maggie so soon after giving birth, so would you like for me to call her husband at home? Then he can notify her brothers."

Aidan sighed and closed his eyes. "I'd be most grateful if you'd do that," he murmured.

She knew the sedative he'd been given would put him to sleep very soon, so she got right to the point. "I'll be happy to, but first I'll need Rosalie's phone number."

He opened his eyes and looked at her blankly, then muttered an oath. "I don't know their number," he groaned. "I don't know any of the kids' numbers. Maggie dials them at home, and my secretary places my calls at the office. I do know that none of them are listed in the phone books."

He thought for a moment. "Wait. I think I have one of Denis's business cards in my wallet. Get it and look through it. I'm sure Denis's card is in there somewhere."

Elizabeth took the billfold out of the drawer in the bedside table and opened it. All but a few dollars of the considerable amount of money he'd carried had been put into the hospital safe, and he had only a few major credit cards, so it didn't take her long to find the somewhat crumpled business card. "That's it," he said, sounding greatly relieved. "It lists both his business and his home phones in Washington. Call him and tell him to get in touch with the others. He has their numbers."

Elizabeth took the card and stared at it, dumbfounded. The last thing she wanted to do was call Denis O'Halloran. She hadn't seen or spoken to him since he'd called off the wedding and walked out of her life on that morning over three years ago. But it was obvious that she had no choice now.

Chapter Two

Hiding her dismay as best she could, Elizabeth stood, then leaned down and kissed Aidan on the forehead. "Go to sleep," she said softly. "I'll take care of it."

He caught her hand between his two bandaged ones and rubbed the back of it against his stubbly cheek. "You've always been like one of our own," he murmured. "That son of mine made the biggest mistake of his life when he let you get away from him. He never found anyone to take your place, either. How could he?"

Elizabeth felt a lump of tears in her throat for what might have been as she gently removed her hand and turned off the lamp, then left the room and shut the door behind her.

It was after eight o'clock when she arrived at the apartment and was greeted by the television showing pictures of the fire, and the familiar aroma of homemade menudo, a spicy Mexican soup. She walked into the kitchen to find Pilar taking a pan of fresh-baked corn bread out of the oven.

"Hi there," she greeted Elizabeth as she set the hot pan on the stove. "Are you just getting off duty? You look beat. I got home about an hour ago. I was just warming up some of the soup I made Friday. Sit down and have some."

Elizabeth sank wearily onto one of the chairs at the table. "Pilar, you're a godsend," she said with a sigh. "I'm sure glad you like to cook. That's one thing I never mastered."

Pilar chuckled. "Yes, I know. I've tasted your efforts, remember?"

She put a bowl of steaming menudo in front of Elizabeth, then heaped squares of corn bread onto a plate and set it on the table before sitting down herself. The volume on the television had been turned up so it could be heard in the kitchen, and the commentator was giving a graphic description of the fire storm that was ravaging the hills of Oakland.

"Are there any figures on how many have been killed and injured?" Elizabeth asked Pilar apprehensively.

The other woman shook her head. "Nothing definite. The numbers change every time they mention them. Sometimes more, sometimes less. Have you had any word about your neighbors up there yet? You know, Deny's parents?"

Elizabeth nodded and told her roommate how she'd spent the past two and a half hours. "According to their charts, Aidan's burns are mostly superficial. Painful but not serious," she said in conclusion. "They'll probably release him tomorrow when his family shows up, but Aunt Maggie looks so drawn and ill. Even with the oxygen, she breathes heavily. Her lung capacity isn't good...."

Elizabeth's voice broke and she ran her fingers through her disheveled hair. Pilar patted her other hand which was curled into a fist on the table beside her plate. "Hey, Liz, those guys in ICU are experts at what they do. They'll see that your Aunt gets the best of care. Why don't you go take a nice long shower and get comfortable, while I do the dishes.''

Elizabeth hoped her gratitude for Pilar's compassion showed in her expression as she looked up. "Oh no," she said emphatically. "You did the cooking, I'll do the cleaning up, but thanks for offering.''

Pilar had lived with Elizabeth long enough to know about her stubborn streak, so she didn't argue. "Okay, if that's the way you want it," she said lightly as she stood, then looked down at Elizabeth with an impishly innocent expression. "Any chance I can stay around and listen in on your conversation with Deny when you call him?''

Elizabeth couldn't help but chuckle as she stood, too. "Nice try, but not the slightest. Now get out of here while I clean up the mess you made.''

Pilar laughed as she turned to leave. "Always happy to oblige," she said, "but you know you're going to tell me about it sooner or later. I don't see why I can't just get it firsthand.''

"In your dreams," Elizabeth sputtered at Pilar's retreating back.

Elizabeth finished in the kitchen and only then did she go into the living room, where the television was reporting the disaster. She watched in horror as the cameras recorded the flaming hell that had been Oakland's most exclusive residential district and her childhood home. The roaring flames and the thick black screen of smoke against the orange wall of fire made it impossible to distinguish anything else. She couldn't concentrate on the accompanying narration as the tears she'd been fighting all day broke loose and streamed down her face.

Dear God, could anything or anyone survive that holocaust? Had her neighborhood been burned out like so many others? Did her parents still have a home? Did Deny's?

Deny. It occurred to her that she was deliberately finding distractions to put off making the call to him, and that was childish. She'd grown up very quickly three years ago, and she didn't intend to slip backward now.

Blinded by tears, she stumbled into the bathroom where she quickly shed her clothes and stood under the warm, tingling spray of the shower until she stopped crying. She'd need a clear head and a firm grip on her emotions when she talked to her ex-fiancé.

Twenty minutes later she wrapped herself in a large bath towel and found the business card in the pocket of the blouse she'd discarded in the clothes hamper. Willing herself to be calm, she headed for the telephone in the kitchen.

After a deep breath, she picked up the phone. Twice she fumbled with the push buttons before finally hearing a ring at the other end. It rang several times before she remembered that it would be past midnight in the East.

A few seconds later a voice as familiar to her as her own answered in a recording and told the caller that he couldn't come to the phone right now but to leave a message and he'd return the call as soon as possible.

The sound of Deny's voice—even a recording—was electrifying, and her hands shook as she listened to it. Damn! She'd tried so hard to believe that he could no longer stir her emotions, and here she was acting like that love-struck teenager she'd been who'd thought he was a super hero, Romeo and God all rolled into one.

She'd reached his answering machine. Apparently he wasn't home. How long would it be before he'd get back to her? Maybe he was out of town or on vacation.

The beep signaled her to start talking and she plunged in. "Deny, this is Elizabeth Kelly. I'm calling to let you know that your parents are safe. Both your mom and dad are in the hospital, but—"

"Elizabeth?" His shouting voice interrupted. "What in hell are you talking about? What's happened?"

She caught her breath. Thank God, he was home, but apparently he hadn't heard about the fire. "Deny, did you listen to the news today?"

"News about what?" He sounded anxious. "Elizabeth, why are you calling me in the middle of the night after three years and four months of refusing to admit that I still exist? And what's this about my parents? Did you say they're in the hospital?"

She felt a quick surge of happiness that he remembered the exact amount of time that had passed since they last saw or talked to each other.

"I'm sorry. I assumed you would have heard by now," she said. "The whole East Hills section of Oakland is on fire."

She heard him gasp, and continued before he could interrupt again. "Your parents escaped, but the smoke caused problems with your mom's emphysema and your dad was burned trying to put out a brushfire. They're both in the hospital, but his burns aren't serious," she hurried to assure him. "Aunt Maggie is being monitored in intensive care, but only until she can breathe normally again without oxygen."

"Oh, my God! Will they be all right? What about your parents?" His voice rang with alarm.

"My parents are vacationing in Greece, but I have no idea whether or not our houses are still standing. The area is closed off. Only firefighters and emergency crews can get in."

"And you? How did you get out of there? Are you all right?" His concern for her was obvious, and she was grateful.

"Oh, I'm fine. I was nowhere near the area when the fire started. I work at Sisters Of Mercy hospital and live downtown now."

"What are you doing working in a hospital? And why are you calling? Not that I don't appreciate your doing so, but where are Rosalie and Finley?" He sounded as if he didn't trust her to get the message straight.

"I'm a nurse, remember? One of the trauma team at the hospital," she told him crisply. "And your sister and brothers aren't available to make the call. Rosalie had her baby yesterday, and Fin is out of town."

"*You're* a nurse with a trauma team?"

Elizabeth knew he'd had a shock, but his incredulous tone touched a hot nerve. "Be quiet, Denis, and listen to me," she snapped. "You made it plain the last time we talked that you think I'm a bubbleheaded incompetent, but I graduated from San Jose State last year with an A average, and I'm a good nurse."

She was ashamed of herself for being so quick to take offense, but his condescension had opened wounds she'd hoped were healed and the pain was sharp.

There was a pregnant silence at the other end, then she heard Deny groan. "Elizabeth, I'm sorry." His tone was thick with contrition. "I'm not thinking straight. I never meant to imply that you are anything but an intelligent, highly competent woman. It's just that hearing your voice on the answering machine after all this time staggered me, and before I could recover from that, you started delivering one shock after the other. Honestly, my head's reeling."

He paused again. "Please forgive me."

She heard the strain in his voice, and hated herself for losing her temper.

It was her turn to apologize. "No, I'm the one who's sorry. Hearing your voice has brought back painful memories for me, too, and I'm not dealing with them well. I just came off an eleven-hour shift at the hospital, I can't find out what's happened to my parents' house, or yours, either, and I'm taking my tiredness and frustration out on you. What do you say we start over again, and I'll try to do better this time?"

"You're not dishing out anything I don't deserve," he said quietly. "Now, when did the fire start?"

She told him everything that had occurred that day—the heat, the wind, the dry hills, and the suddenness with which the fire roared into an inferno. She described the scene at the hospital when casualties crowded and overpowered the emergency room and overflowed into the rest of the medical center.

"It wasn't until early evening that your dad recognized me as I passed him in the hall," she said, and described their reunion at the hospital, her search for Maggie, and their visit with her in ICU.

"I read her chart, Deny, and there are no burns or bruises," she concluded, hoping to allay his anxiety. "As of now, her distress is confined to her emphysema plus smoke inhalation. Of course, with her already damaged lungs there could be complications, but she's getting the best of care and the prognosis is good for a complete recovery. Call the hospital yourself, they'll give you a report on her condition. Also turn on your television. Any of the news stations will have coverage."

"I intend to do both," he said. "And I'll catch the first flight out of here in the morning."

Deny was coming back to Oakland! He'd be spending time at the same hospital where she worked. Would he want to see her? Did she want to see him?

"I think that's wise," she told him. "They need their family with them at a time like this. The fire's still not under control, and we're shorthanded in the trauma center, but I'll keep an eye on them until someone in your family shows up to take over."

"I . . . I don't know how I can ever make you understand how much this means to me." There was a tremor in his voice.

She didn't want his gratitude. The last thing she needed was for him to think he owed her.

"Aunt Maggie and Uncle Aidan are very dear to me," she said. "I'll do everything I can for them, but if you want to help, you can phone your brothers and sister and tell them where your parents are. Aidan doesn't remember their unlisted numbers."

"Of course, I'll do it right away."

"Yes, by all means," she said. "I'm sure they're frantic by now, so I'll hang up and clear your line. Goodbye, Deny. I hope the firefighters were able to save your home."

"Wait!" she heard him say as she put the phone back in its cradle. She had nothing more to say to Denis O'Halloran. It would be a mistake to get involved with him again, even on a short-term basis. They'd been too close all their lives to ever be casual friends. She'd suffered long and painfully over their breakup, but now she'd come to terms with it and could even admit that it had been for the best.

She was happy with the work she was doing and the life she was living. Someday she wanted to fall in love once more, but not with Deny. He'd hurt her too deeply and humiliated her too publicly to ever trust him again!

Elizabeth went to sleep almost as soon as she crawled into bed and closed her eyes, and didn't wake up until her clock radio clicked on at five the next morning with the news. The commentator announced that the fire was now under control but still burning. Property damage in the millions, there were thousands homeless, and the count was still soaring. How the fire had started was unknown, and the possibility of arson was being investigated.

Elizabeth shuddered as she crawled out of bed and headed for the bathroom. Surely nobody would do such a monstrous thing as to deliberately set those woodlands ablaze. After five years of drought and a killing frost the winter before, the trees and brush were dry and flamed up like tinder.

Twenty minutes later Elizabeth was dressed and ready to face another hectic day. She usually wore slacks and a blouse to work, then changed into the green cotton scrub uniform she wore on duty in the emergency area. This morning she'd chosen jeans and a blue-and-white-striped T-shirt.

Pilar was already in the kitchen, measuring coffee beans into the coffeemaker, when Elizabeth walked in. The small radio on the counter was turned to the same station she'd been listening to in her room, and she arrived in time to hear the latest casualty statistics report of ten dead and more than fifty people treated for burns and smoke inhalation in area hospitals.

"I'm afraid that's just the tip of the iceberg," Pilar said grimly as she plugged in the coffeepot. "I'll bet we treated that many injured at Sisters of Mercy alone yesterday."

Elizabeth nodded and put slices of bread in the toaster. "I agree. It seemed like an unending line. I'm heading over to the hospital a little early this morning so I can look in on the O'Hallorans."

"So how did your conversation with Deny go last night?" Pilar asked with her usual brash curiosity.

Elizabeth shrugged. "How could it go? I had bad news to tell him and he was upset. He hadn't heard about the fire, and it was a real shock to him. He's flying in sometime today."

"Are you looking forward to seeing him?" Pilar probed. "He's not married, is he?"

The toast popped up with a loud click and Elizabeth jumped. "No, he's not married," she said as she reached for the butter, "and I don't plan to see him. It's been over between us for a long time."

Pilar looked at her searchingly. "Okay, if you say so, but as soon as things around here get back to normal, I want to hear the whole story of that breakup."

Half an hour later Elizabeth arrived at the hospital, changed into her scrubs and climbed the flight of stairs to the intensive care area on the second floor. Outside, the wind still blew, and a blackish-brown curtain of smoke covered the sky, hiding the dawn and clogging the air with eye-burning, lung-searing pollutants.

At the monitoring station she was told that Maggie's respiration was good and she was sleeping peacefully. Elizabeth walked over to the cubicle to check for herself. She was relieved to find Maggie breathing much easier, although still with the aid of the oxygen.

Upstairs, on the third floor, she found Aidan awake and impatient. "Those damn nurses insist that I stay in bed, and then they won't answer my light," he grumbled as soon as she walked into the room.

"They're awfully busy," she assured him. "Is there something I can do for you?"

"Yes," he snapped. "Find out how Maggie is and come and tell me. If I don't hear from you in ten minutes I'm going down there myself even if I have to wander through the halls in this cockamamy nightshirt that leaves my rear end exposed."

Elizabeth only barely stifled a laugh. This was the Uncle Aidan she knew, and she was delighted to welcome him back, temper and all. It was no wonder the nurses were slow to answer his light. As CEO of one of the biggest banking institutions in California, Aidan O'Halloran barked orders, wanted everything done yesterday and could be a real tyrant if his demands weren't followed.

"I'm sure you have the cutest bottom in the hospital, but it won't be necessary to show it off," she assured him with a teasing smile. "I've just come from ICU and Maggie's fine. She's still asleep, her vital signs are good, and although she's still getting oxygen, her breathing is normal. Now, let's talk about you. Are you getting pain medication for those burns?"

He relaxed and sighed. "Yeah. I'm fine, but I need some clothes. I'm checking out as soon as the doctor comes."

Elizabeth's sense of relief was short-lived. "Don't go making any plans before that," she warned anxiously. "He may not feel you're ready to be released."

"They can't keep me here if I don't want to stay," Aidan fumed. "The nurse told me when she was here earlier that several of the kids had called to ask how I was and to say they'd be here this morning. What time is it?"

Elizabeth looked at her watch. "It's almost six o'clock, and I'm going to have to get down to my station in a few minutes."

"Don't be in such a hurry," he said petulantly. "I want to know what Denis said last night when you called him?"

Elizabeth nodded. "When I told him about the fire, he was very upset," she told Aidan. "He hadn't heard about it. I filled him in as best I could, and he said he'd catch the first flight out today."

"Was he...was he surprised to hear it from you? Or...uh...have you been in touch at other times?" Aidan kept his gaze down, as though uncomfortable looking at her directly.

He had good reason to sense that he was touching on a subject she didn't want to discuss. "Yes, he was surprised," she said shortly. "I haven't seen or talked to him since he called off the wedding, and what's more I don't want to. I'm going to ask a favor of you, Uncle Aidan."

He looked at her then. "Anything. All you have to do is tell me what it is you want. You must know that."

She nodded and pressed her lips together to keep them from trembling. "If you know my address or telephone number I don't want you to give them to Deny, and I'd appreciate it if you don't talk to him about me."

Aidan frowned. "But he'll be spending a lot of time here at the hospital as long as his mother is here. You're bound to run into him."

"No. I'll make sure that I don't. Besides, she'll probably be released later today or maybe tomorrow. After that she'll have her own family to look after her."

A flash of pain contorted his face. "Maggie and I have always thought of you as part of our family—another daughter, Elizabeth."

Elizabeth blinked back the insistent tears that seemed to lurk just behind her eyes. "Please, Uncle Aidan, don't make me cry." It was part plea, part wail.

Aiden muttered an oath and caught her hand in his bandaged one. "Ah, lass, I'm sorry. I'm being a selfish old fool. Of course I'll honor your request. Besides, I don't know your address or phone number. If Denis wants to see you he'll have to find you himself.''

For a moment they were both silent, then she leaned down and kissed him. "I really do have to run now. I'll look in on you again later this morning."

"I won't be here. I'll be down with Maggie, so come there."

She sighed and patted his cheek. "Be good now, Uncle Aidan, and follow the doctor's orders. If he says you're not ready to be released then believe him. He knows what he's talking about."

"I'm checking myself out," he said adamantly. "Maggie needs me."

At the trauma center the pace wasn't as wild as it had been yesterday, but neither was it peaceful. They were still bringing in casualties from the fire, but not as many. The evacuation had been completed, but the area was still sealed off.

It was after ten o'clock before Elizabeth was able to take a short break, and she hurried up to the intensive care unit. True to his word, Aidan was in the waiting room. His hands and arms were bandaged a little less heavily now, and he was wearing clean slacks and a short-sleeved sport shirt, so apparently one of his sons had brought him new clothes.

Finley, the third of Aidan and Maggie's sons, was with his father, and he reached for Elizabeth, lifted her off the floor and hugged her. It was like being reunited with an older brother. All Deny's brothers had treated her the same as they treated their sister, Rosalie, and Elizabeth alternately loved and loathed the three of them the same way Rosie did, but the fourth son, Deny, had been special.

"Hey, Elizabeth, you haven't changed a bit," Fin teased. "I'll bet you still don't weigh a hundred pounds. Jeez, but it's good to see you."

She laughed but looked around anxiously, relieved to see that there was no one but O'Hallorans in the room who might be disturbed by their boisterous reunion. "Finley O'Halloran, you great oaf," she squealed, and hugged him back. "It's wonderful to see you, too, and I'll have you know I weigh one hundred and three pounds. Now put me down before you squash me."

She was exaggerating, of course. Although Fin was big, six feet five inches and a great basketball player in college, he was also gentle and handled her with loving care.

"Okay, Thumbelina," he said as he stood her back on the floor, "but don't give me any more of your sass or I'll stuff you in my backpack and take you home to Lucy."

"And how is your lovely wife? And the kids? Are they all in school now?"

"Lucy's great, and all the kids are in school except the twins."

Elizabeth's eyes widened with surprise. "Twins! When did that happen?"

He grinned proudly. "Daniel and Donald will be one year old in December."

Before she could congratulate Fin, his older brother, Glendon, strolled in. He glanced at her, then did a double take and beamed. "Elizabeth! I didn't recognize you." He, too, grabbed her in a bear hug, and she threw her arms around his neck. "Dad said you were a nurse now, but I guess I still expected to see a young college girl. Damn, you're all grown-up!"

She laughed. "It had to happen sometime. How are you, Glen? Do you still have the gallery in South Lake Tahoe?"

Glendon was the second O'Halloran son. Several inches shorter than Finley, he was a well-known artist.

He released her and nodded, but before he could answer, Aidan interrupted. "How's your mother? Have they said anything about moving her out of intensive care yet?"

Glendon shook his head. "No. They kicked me out so they could give her a bath, but she seems quite perky." He looked at Elizabeth. "She asked about you. She wants to see you."

"I want to see her, too, and I only have a few minutes before I have to be back on the floor. If you'll excuse me, I'll run in and say hello while she's being bathed."

When in her green uniform, Elizabeth was free to enter any area of the hospital, and she hurried to the cubicle. Another nurse had finished bathing Maggie and had helped her into a fresh nightgown. Maggie was sitting in a chair while the nurse changed her bed.

"Elizabeth," Maggie said with a big smile as Elizabeth kissed her on the cheek and sat down beside her. "How are you? Oh, it's so good to see you again."

She still had the oxygen cannula in her nose, but her color was much better today, and she sounded only slightly breathless. "It's just great to see you sitting up, Aunt Maggie," Elizabeth said, "but I'm sorry we had to meet again under these circumstances."

Maggie's smile disappeared. "Yes," she said sadly. "I know your parents are away so they're safe, but have you been able to reach them to tell them about the fire."

Elizabeth shook her head. "No, I haven't even tried. They're touring Greece with a group of amateur archaeologists, and I have no idea how to get in touch with them. Of course, this certainly qualifies as an emergency, so I could go through the travel agency and have them located. But I'm not going to. There's nothing they can do, and I see no reason to spoil their vacation just yet. If they hear about it over there they'll call me. Meanwhile, I've talked to the insurance people and Dad's lawyers. They're investigating."

Maggie nodded thoughtfully. "I see your reasoning, and I agree. Let Kathleen and Connor enjoy themselves before they have to come back to this terrible devastation. Have you heard anything about the houses yet?"

"No, and I don't imagine we will for a while. They won't let anyone in there until the fire is out and everything's cooled down. You and Uncle Aidan are safe, though, and that's what matters most."

Maggie nodded thoughtfully. "You're right, of course, but I can't help thinking of all our things..."

Elizabeth knew she'd better change the subject quickly. "Worrying won't change anything, and right now you need to concentrate on getting well. Oh, and congratulations, I understand you have a new grandson."

Maggie's smile returned. "Yes. We were at the hospital when he was born. Weighed almost nine pounds, and you could tell from the way he howled that there was nothing wrong with his lungs. Rosalie's husband, Vic, came to see me early this morning. He says he'll be taking his wife and baby home this afternoon."

Elizabeth looked at her watch. "That's great. Look, I'm going to have to run. We're still awfully busy downstairs."

She started to stand, but Maggie reached out and stopped her. "Aidan says you're the one who called Denis last night. Is everything all right?"

"Oh, yes," she said warily. "He hadn't heard about the fire, so he was shocked and worried about you, but otherwise he seemed to be fine—"

"I don't mean with him," Maggie interrupted. "I mean with you. Will you two be...I mean, will you be seeing him? He'll be here around noon."

Even to spare Maggie heartache, she couldn't pretend that she and Deny could be friends again.

"No, Aunt Maggie," she said firmly. "We won't be seeing each other. There's no point in it, and it would just stir up painful memories."

As if they hadn't already been stirred up, she thought.

She stood, then leaned down and kissed the top of Maggie's head. "I promise to make sure you're well taken care of, and I'll see you again before you leave the hospital."

She left, and after stopping to say a quick goodbye to the men in the waiting room, she hurried on downstairs. The last thing she wanted was to run into Deny should he arrive a little early.

The rest of the morning was hectic, but from what she could glean from overheard snatches of conversation as she rushed from incoming ambulances to examining rooms, the fire had been completely controlled and all but a few hot spots extinguished.

By noon she was becoming anxious. Deny would be arriving at the hospital soon if he wasn't there already, and her heart and mind were at odds with each other. She told herself she didn't want to see him, but still she looked up hopefully every few minutes, thinking she'd heard his voice.

At her lunch break she got a ham sandwich and a cola out of the vending machines and took them into the nurses' lounge. She usually ate in the cafeteria, but didn't want to risk running into him there.

During a lull in midafternoon she called ICU and was told that Maggie had been moved into a private room on the medical floor. That meant she was on the road to recovery. Hopefully the following day she'd be released from the hospital and Elizabeth could relax on that score.

* * *

Unfortunately, for both Elizabeth and Maggie, the course of events didn't run that smoothly.

When Elizabeth arrived at the hospital early Tuesday morning, she called the nursing station on Maggie's floor to ask about her and was told that she'd been returned to ICU.

"Oh, no!" Elizabeth gasped. "What happened?"

"She developed respiratory problems during the night and was moved to intensive care where she could be more closely monitored," the nurse informed her.

Knowing she couldn't get any further information on the phone, Elizabeth hung up. Then she asked another nurse to cover for her while she hurried up to the second floor. She looked around cautiously as she stepped out of the elevator. To her relief there was no sign of Deny. The family was probably in the waiting room at the other end of the hall.

Again she hesitated when she entered the intensive care section, and scanned the area before approaching the nurses' station. She saw Aidan standing beside the bed in one of the cubicles and knew she was safe for a while. Only one visitor was allowed at a time in here.

She walked over to the desk and asked to see Maggie's chart. A quick glance showed that Maggie had developed lobar pneumonia, one of the complications they'd hoped to avoid. Her temperature had spiked, and she was back on oxygen full-time. A serious though not unusual development.

Elizabeth headed for the cubicle, and Aidan looked up as she slipped in to stand on the other side of the bed. Maggie's eyes were closed, and she looked flushed and restless. Even with the oxygen, her breathing was somewhat labored.

Aidan put his finger to his lips, then motioned Elizabeth to come with him as he turned to leave. She saw that he looked tired and drawn when they paused in the anteroom, where they could talk without disturbing anyone.

"Thank you for coming," he said in a tone as grim as his expression. "Can you tell me what happened? She seemed to be doing so well yesterday. The doctor isn't around and I can't get much out of the nurses."

"Pneumonia is always a danger in respiratory illnesses, Uncle Aidan. I won't tell you it's nothing to be concerned about, but it's seldom fatal anymore."

He muttered an expletive. "They never should have taken her out of intensive care yesterday," he fumed.

She put her hand on his arm and signaled him to lower his voice. "Because of the emergency, there is a shortage of beds in here, but her vital signs were good and she was being closely monitored on the medical floor. I've read her chart, and it's really not as bad as it looks to you. She's getting the best available care and medication, and Maggie's a fighter. Please, try not to worry so."

"Easy to say," he grumbled. "You're coming to the waiting room to say hello to Seamus and Jill, aren't you? You haven't seen them yet. They're here from Carmel."

She hesitated. "Is Deny here?"

He looked straight at her. "Yes, he is. He wants to see you."

She could feel her expression harden. "You know how I feel. Please don't interfere."

He slumped visibly. "You know I won't, but I wish you'd just talk to him. He was upset when I insisted that he leave you alone and wait for you to come to him if you wanted to."

Elizabeth felt a wave of emotion, but wasn't sure whether it was relief or regret. "I'm sorry you've been caught in the middle of this," she said gently.

"But what about later?" he asked anxiously. "Will you stay in touch with Maggie and me?"

"Yes, of course," she said, but knew it would never be the same. Much as she loved the O'Hallorans, the two families had been wrenched apart too violently to ever again be free and easy with one another.

Chapter Three

Denis O'Halloran paced restlessly around the small crowded hospital waiting room. He'd been tense and anxious ever since that totally unexpected middle-of-the-night phone call from Elizabeth. Just hearing her voice after all this time had rattled him to a disturbing degree, and then when she'd told him about the fire and his mother....

He stopped at the doorway and leaned against it, watching the conglomeration of people coming and going in the halls. He'd always been uncomfortable in hospitals and avoided them if possible, but now...

His musing was interrupted by the sight of his father and a nurse in a green uniform coming out of the ICU at the other end of the hall. It took him only a second to realize that the nurse was Elizabeth Anne Kelly!

His Elizabeth. The little girl with the mass of red curls that had tumbled in disarray around her head and down her back. The petite teenager with marvelous big blue eyes, and a musical laugh that sang on the wind. The very young bride-to-be with the loving touch and lips that trembled under his.

He shifted uncomfortably but couldn't take his hungry gaze off her as she and Aidan stopped in front of the elevator. She hadn't changed at all in looks. Her hair was still bright flaming red with sparkling gold highlights, and she was still small, but with full breasts, tiny waist and rounded hips that couldn't be disguised even by the shapeless uniform she wore.

But there was something different about her. Her hair was shorter and tamer, but it wasn't so much her looks as her manner. Her bearing was more dignified as she stood quietly talking to his father. He could tell from their phone conversation Sunday night that she'd matured a great deal since he'd last seen her. The self-centered, impetuous child, sparkling with happiness that he'd so effectively destroyed three years ago, seemed to have been replaced by a young professional woman with an air of competence and dedication.

How like her. She'd never done anything halfway. Sure she'd been spoiled. An only child, her wealthy parents had been in their forties when she was born. How could she not have been spoiled? But she'd also been extravagantly generous with her love and compassion. She'd fed and sheltered every stray kitten and puppy in need of care, and cleaned and bandaged all the cuts and bruises of her playmates, as well as provide them a shoulder to cry on when they were hurting.

It wasn't surprising that she'd chosen trauma nursing as a profession. She'd been born to heal the sick in both body and spirit.

A knot of self-disgust formed in his belly and spread. He'd really done a hatchet job on her when he'd called off their wedding, but that had never been his intention. He hadn't wanted to break up with her, just postpone the marriage until they were both more mature.

They'd grown up next door to each other and had never been apart. As children they'd played together, as adolescents she'd been his steady girl, and as college students they'd been lovers. They'd never had a chance to find out who they were individually because they'd always been a couple, an extension of each other.

All he'd wanted was a little space to grow and find his place in the order of things before he settled down with a wife and the family that would follow. He'd wanted Elizabeth to have a chance to grow up, too, and to wean herself away from her hovering parents who had still thought of her as a child who needed to be led around by the hand.

But he'd botched it as badly as anyone could have. Though it was only three years ago, he looked back and saw a much younger man—a boy almost—in his place. The words had come out all wrong, and the longer he talked the worse it got. She'd looked so stricken, and he'd felt like the lowest form of life. In the end she'd renounced him completely.

It didn't get any better after he'd arrived in Washington, alone and a stranger in a strange town. He'd taken Elizabeth for granted because she was always there for him. He'd had no idea how much he was going to miss her after he'd cut the cord that bound them, and set himself adrift.

By the time he'd fully realized the depth of his feelings, it was too late to go back and plead for her forgiveness. The wedding had been called off and the two families were involved in a full-scale war of accusations and recriminations. He'd written and phoned in an effort to undo at least some of the damage he'd caused to their relationship, but Elizabeth refused to take his phone calls and sent his letters back unopened.

The flash of the red light above the elevator doors caught his eye, and he watched as she went so naturally into his father's arms and hugged him before the doors opened and she stepped inside.

Deny's whole body ached for that hug. He'd sell his soul if he could go back three years and four months and do things differently, if by some miracle he could earn the right to just hold her again.

When Elizabeth returned to the apartment after work, there was a message on their answering machine from her insurance agent telling her that residents would be allowed to go into the burned area anytime after eight o'clock the following morning. "I have to warn you that it's unlikely your house is still standing," he said carefully. "That whole section of the district was pretty well wiped out. It's all ashes and water and mud, so wear old clothes and heavy-soled shoes. There will be parking below, but you may have to hike up into the hills. Call me afterward, and we'll set up an appointment to go over your losses."

Even though she'd known it was unlikely that her family home would escape the flames, she felt as though the breath had been knocked out of her. She slumped against the counter that separated the kitchen from the living room.

A sympathetic arm across her shoulder alerted her that Pilar had come up behind her and heard the recorded message. "God, Liz, I'm so sorry. Do you want me to go with you tomorrow?"

Elizabeth ran her fingers through her thick curls and shook her head. "Thanks, Pilar, but I'll be okay, and you're needed at the hospital. Tomorrow's my day off, and I'll probably spend the afternoon with the insurance people."

She smiled shakily. "I appreciate the offer, though. You're a good friend."

"Don't forget, I know what it's like to be homeless," Pilar reminded her. "I spent my childhood migrating with my parents from one farm to another in search of crops to pick. We never had a home, just a series of shacks to eat and sleep in until the work ran out.

"Actually, that was probably better than having one and losing it," she mused. "At least I never became attached to any of those flimsy hovels."

She hugged Elizabeth then stepped back. "Now, how about if I fix dinner while you take a shower and relax a little? Wait till you taste my chili. It'll take your mind off your troubles."

Pilar was right. The chili took Elizabeth's mind off her troubles and centered it on her burning tongue and stomach. It was delicious, but *hot!* "Good heavens," she exclaimed as she sucked on a large ice cube from her water glass. "Did you really mean to make it this hot?"

Pilar hooted with laughter. "That's nothing. You should taste my mother's." She stood and started clearing the dishes from the table. "I have frozen yogurt for dessert, that'll cool you off. Let's take it in the living room where we can be more comfortable while you tell me all about what happened after Denis O'Halloran called off your wedding three years ago."

"While I what?" Elizabeth gasped.

"Oh, come on, Liz." Pilar's pout was only half-teasing. "You said you'd tell me about it later, and that was two days ago. You can't leave me hanging. You know what a buttinsky I am."

"Yes, ma'am, I certainly do know," Elizabeth said sternly, but she couldn't resist a half smile. "However, since I brought the subject up in the first place I guess you're entitled to know the whole story. You dish up the frozen yogurt, and I'll get the iced tea."

Several minutes later the two women were settled on the beige velour sofa with their dessert, and Elizabeth began reluctantly reciting the painful events of her canceled marriage ceremony.

"It was June, just a week before the wedding was scheduled to take place," she said haltingly as she strove to put her thoughts in order. "It was to be an extravaganza with no expense spared, and for weeks Deny and I had been feted at showers, and luncheons, and dinners until we'd piled up enough gifts to fill two rooms when they were displayed."

Elizabeth shuddered even now as she remembered how painful it had been to repackage all those items and return them.

"It was Saturday morning and I was upstairs in my bedroom having the final fitting on my wedding gown. Our housekeeper came up to tell me that Deny was in the library and wanted to talk to me. I hadn't been expecting him, but I was too happy and excited to be concerned."

As Elizabeth recounted the scene it was as if she were living it over again. She could actually smell the fragrance from the vases of spring flowers newly cut and brought in from the garden, and hear herself humming the wedding march as she rushed into the library and flung herself into Deny's arms.

"Hey, what are you doing here?" she'd asked as she hugged him. "I thought you had another fitting on your tuxedo this morning."

She'd tipped her head up for a kiss, but it was perfunctory rather than passionate.

"I canceled it," he said, and his voice had an odd quality about it that jarred her.

She opened her eyes and looked at him. God, but he was gorgeous! He wasn't that tall, but just right for her. She could put her arms around his muscular shoulders without having to stand on a stool.

"You mean postponed it," she said, "but, Deny, you shouldn't have done that. There's not much time left for the tailor to make alterations if necessary."

He shook his head and released her, and for the first time she noticed the pinched look on his handsome face and the anxiety in his deep blue eyes.

"No, Elizabeth, I mean canceled." He paused and drew a deep breath. "I'm taking the job in Washington."

She'd blinked, then blinked again as the full force of his words registered. "What on earth are you talking about? You're reporting for work at Dover Oil Company in San Francisco the Monday after we return from our honeymoon. It's all settled."

He met her gaze head-on. "I'm sorry but I'm not taking the job with Dover. It doesn't have the career possibilities that the one in Washington offers. I've already notified them."

She couldn't believe what she was hearing. "But that job requires traveling. You'd be out of the country for weeks at a time."

"I'm aware of that," he said carefully. "It would mean postponing the rest of your education for a few years so you could travel with me, but would that be so bad? You could always go back and get your degree in two or three years when my job is more stationary."

Two or three years seemed like a lifetime to Elizabeth. "I just don't believe this," she said. "You promised we'd stay close to home. I told you, I don't want to leave Dad and Mom to live thousands of miles away. I'm all the family they've got. We talked it over and you agreed with me."

"Not agreed," he said sadly. "I capitulated like I did with the plans for an obscenely expensive wedding when I'd have preferred a small, intimate ceremony with family and a few close friends. But now that I've had time to think it over, I know that this time I have to do what's best for me.

"I've worked hard for my degree in chemical engineering and I intend to make the most of it. My opportunities with the government are limitless, but I can't wait around for several years until you grow up enough to leave mommy and daddy and be my wife."

She stared at him, feeling betrayed and angry. "That's a rotten thing to say. Your parents have four other children, all living within a couple of hundred miles of them, but I'm all Mother and Dad have. I don't want to leave them."

He turned away. "You're all I have, too, but you aren't giving any consideration to what I want."

"That's not true!" she gasped. "I love you, but it's different with you. You graduated at the top of your class. You've had plenty of job offers. Dover is one of the biggest oil companies in the country, and the pay was better than what the government offered."

He turned back to face her, and she saw his strained expression. "We both know that the money isn't that important. I was hoping that once we were married, your home would be where I was, not where your parents are."

She caught her breath. Why was he doing this? Why hadn't he at least talked it over with her again before accepting the government position?

"I don't understand," she said. "If a small wedding and the job in Washington were so important to you, why didn't you say so?"

He nodded sadly. "I did, Elizabeth. I told you exactly how I felt, but you just shrugged it off and went on with your own plans. Or rather, whatever your parents planned."

She couldn't believe he'd think that. She remembered him mentioning that he thought they could keep the wedding simpler, but their parents were the ones planning it. She'd just gone along with what they wanted and assumed he'd speak to them if he really objected to their arrangements.

As for the job, they'd discussed it at length. It's true that he'd seemed really excited about the chance to work for that department, but frankly the thought of moving so far away from her family and friends terrified her. Her parents had always sheltered and protected her, and she wasn't ready yet to give up that safe harbor.

She'd explained all this to Deny and he'd understood. Or at least he'd agreed not to take her so far away from home. Why had he changed his mind at the last minute?

"If you think I'm so immature and insensitive then why did you ask me to marry you?" she said haltingly.

"Because I love you," he answered, and she felt a wave of relief until he added, "and also because it was expected of me. If you'll remember, our parents were always making sly remarks about when were we going to announce the engagement, or wasn't it about time we started thinking about a commitment now that I was in my last year of college."

Elizabeth was shaken all the way to her toes. Was he telling her he'd only asked her to marry him to please their families? But that couldn't be. They'd grown up knowing that someday they'd take those sacred vows. Even as small children they'd played house, he was the husband and she the wife.

Maybe he was just having last-minute jitters before taking the big step. She'd heard that was a pretty common reaction for men as the wedding day approached. Probably all he needed was a little cajoling.

Closing the gap between them, she put her arms around his waist and snuggled against him. "You know what I think?" she asked softly. "I think we're both exhausted from the strain we've been under, and we're saying things we don't really mean. I didn't intend to disregard your wishes for a smaller wedding. I honestly didn't realize it was so important to you, but it's too late to do anything about that now. As for the job in Washington...we've already promised my parents that we'll stay in this area. Besides, if I wait several years, I may have trouble getting into a nursing program unless I take some classes over again."

A look of pain that he made no effort to hide flashed across his face. "I know it would be a big sacrifice, but no more than the one that you're asking me to make." He spoke so low that it took her a moment to catch what he was saying. "I don't expect you to do it. That's why I canceled my fitting for the tux. I won't be needing it."

A stab of fear caught her in the midsection, but she ignored it and kept her voice firm. "Of course you'll be needing it. The wedding is next Saturday."

Slowly he disentangled her from him and walked away. "No, love, it's not. I took so long making up my mind to accept the position that they'd tentatively selected someone else. The other person hadn't been notified yet so I can still have the job, but it means catching a flight out of San Francisco tomorrow night for Washington in order to start work on Monday. Since you won't come with me, I'm afraid that means the wedding is off."

Elizabeth felt the blood drain from her head, and her knees began to shake as she sank down onto the chair nearest her. Dear God, he really meant it! Why was he being so obstinate? Surely he couldn't honestly want to leave his hometown, his family, his friends, to live and work thousands of miles away in a strange city where they knew nobody.

She clutched the wooden arms of the high-backed chair with trembling hands and hoped she could control her voice. "We can't postpone the wedding. The invitations were sent out weeks ago. The church date is reserved, and then there's the music, the flowers and the caterers for the reception. The bridesmaids' gowns have already been delivered.''

He stood a few feet away looking down at her, and when he spoke she knew she was in trouble. "You don't understand. I'm not suggesting that we postpone the wedding for a few weeks. I'm saying there will be no wedding until we're both sure it's what we want and not just what our parents expect.''

She stared at him blankly, too shocked to respond, until an unthinkable suspicion exploded in her mind. "There's someone else, isn't there?'' Her tone was as blank as her stare.

Deny blinked. "What do you mean?''

"Just what I said," she responded impatiently as she stood. "You're in love with another woman.''

The anger she'd been too numb to feel before was building now. "My God, Deny, I may be slow but I'm not stupid. Why didn't you just tell me that in the first place instead of all this prattle about finding out who we are.…''

"There's no other woman!'' Deny hadn't raised his voice, but the cold fury behind it effectively silenced Elizabeth. "You know that as well as I do. I'm not going to waste my time and breath denying it further.''

For some inexplicable reason she believed him. Her assumption had been a reasonable one, but when he denied it she knew him so well that she had no doubt about his truthfulness.

On the other hand, she certainly wasn't going to apologize!

"All right," she said, and sat back down. "I'll accept that, but then why are you doing this? Are you just trying to scare me into going East with you?''

He ran his fingers through his thick black hair. "No, Elizabeth, I'm not trying to coerce you into going with me. Ever since we first talked about it I've known that if I went, I'd go alone. That's why it's taken me so long to come to a decision. When I accepted the position I knew it meant we wouldn't be getting married."

She was too shocked to react. Instead, she sat gripping the arms of the chair and staring at him. A wave of dizziness set off a roaring in her head, and she struggled frantically to maintain her equilibrium.

She felt Deny's hand on her arm and the roaring stopped. "Sweetheart, are you all right?" He sounded deeply concerned.

She managed to focus her gaze on him and saw that he was hunkered down beside the chair. "Honey, please try to understand," he pleaded. "I love you. I always have, but you're simply not ready yet for marriage. I don't think I am, either. We both need time to find out who we are as individuals."

"I already know who I am." Her tone was ragged.

"No, you don't," he argued gently. "You're still Mama's little girl. You won't be an adult, no matter how old you grow, until you cut those satin apron strings and start making your own decisions. I know what I'm talking about. It took me a long time, but I finally woke up to the fact that our parents have been pushing us toward marriage all our lives. It was what they wanted, and they never gave a thought about what might be best for us."

She looked at him through eyes clouded with anguish. "That's not true! It's not as if we've never dated other people. You had other girlfriends when I was still too young to go out with boys. And while we were in separate colleges we both dated different people. But our relationship was . . . is . . . special. We're best friends. We wanted to be together.''

Deny stood and began pacing. ''Yes, we've always been best friends. I hope we always will be. But maybe we spent so much time together because that's the way we were taught. We had the run of each other's homes. Our families took vacations together. You even call my parents Aunt Maggie and Uncle Aidan, and yours are Aunt Kathleen and Uncle Connor to me.''

It sounded like gibberish to Elizabeth. ''Our families are close. What's wrong with that?''

''Nothing is wrong with it. But sometimes too much closeness can be suffocating. Don't you see, honey? We need time apart to find out if what we feel is truly romantic love or a close family bond. I'm proposing that you stay here for the next two years and finish school while I go to Washington and get settled in my job. By the end of that time we should be mature enough to know whether or not we want to spend the rest of our lives together. If we marry now and find out later it was a mistake we'd be miserable all the rest of our lives. We both take vows made before God seriously, and divorce is not an option for us.''

She could see that he'd given this a lot of thought. Obviously he had strong doubts about his love for her, and she was too stunned and aggrieved to counter with an equally strong case for the certainty of her love for him.

In that moment she knew that her dreams for the future had come crashing down around her. No matter how much she loved Deny she wasn't going to plead with him to marry her. He may have shattered her belief in Cinderella and Prince Charming and happy ever after, but she still had some pride. It might be a cold thing to snuggle up to in bed, but it just might get her through the next few minutes. Or hours. Or days.

Clasping her hands in her lap to keep them from trembling, she looked straight ahead. "I can't force you to go through with this wedding." Her voice only wavered slightly. "I wouldn't, even if I could, but neither am I going to wait around for two years while you make up your mind whether or not you want me."

"Elizabeth, you—"

She rose then and walked over to stand in front of him as she worked the diamond engagement ring off her finger. "Here," she said, and held it out to him. "I'm giving you your freedom, but I want one thing in return. I don't ever want to see or hear from you again. Now please get out of here and leave me alone."

It seemed to her that his already pale face went even whiter. "Honey, you can't mean that. I know what I'm doing is despicable. I'm a first-class bastard to put you in this difficult and embarrassing position, but even so it's better than a risky marriage."

"Oh, but I do mean it," she said, and reached for his hand. It was cold, although the day was hot. She put the ring into his palm and closed his fingers over it. "You're right about one thing. You *are* a bastard, and I don't want you for a husband, sweetheart, or friend."

For a moment his gaze held hers, and she somehow managed to return it without blinking. Then he turned and walked toward the door. "I'm sorry, Elizabeth. I can't tell you how sorry. I'll ask Mom to hire a couple of secretaries to help you notify the guests and return the presents, and I'll send Aunt Kathleen a check to cover the expense of canceling everything."

He'd opened the door then turned to look at her again. He'd started to raise his arms as if to beckon her to him, then dropped them back to his sides.

"It tears me up to do this to you, sweetheart." His tone had been gentle and there'd been anguish in his eyes. "I'm going to miss you more than I dare think about...."

His voice had broken and he'd quickly stepped outside and shut the door behind him, leaving her standing there with her heart as mangled as her silly romantic dreams.

Elizabeth paused at this point in her story and dragged her thoughts into the present. She set her melted yogurt on the coffee table and looked at Pilar. "I grew up very quickly in that moment," she murmured sadly, "but by then it was too late. By the time Mom came looking for me in the library after Deny left I was hysterical. When I told her what had happened, she immediately called Dad. He rushed home, listened to my story, and went storming next door bent on mayhem of some sort. Deny wasn't there and Dad and Uncle Aidan got into a shouting match instead.

"Mom was so outraged that she said a lot of nasty things to Aunt Maggie about her 'no good' son, which raised Maggie's ire and pretty soon everyone was accusing everyone else. The strong, deep friendship our families had treasured was ruined. Since then they have had nothing to do with one another. Even though they continued to live next door, they speak only when it is unavoidable."

Elizabeth went on to say that her parents refused the O'Hallorans' offer to pay the expenses that remained even though the wedding was canceled. The O'Hallorans wanted to help notify guests and return gifts, but her parents refused that offer, as well. "Instead, I did it all. It took most of the summer, and was the most heartbreaking and embarrassing experience that could possibly happen," she told Pilar as she fought to keep her voice from breaking. "I doubt that anyone has been more publicly humiliated than I was...."

This time her voice did break, and she choked back a sob. "Although I never told anyone the details, it was common knowledge that Deny had walked out on me."

Pilar muttered an unladylike oath. "Oh, Liz, how awful. What did you do?"

Elizabeth took a deep breath and shrugged. "The only thing I could do. I went back to school that fall and studied hard to become a good nurse."

"And you haven't seen or talked to Deny since?"

Elizabeth shook her head. "No, and I don't intend to start again now. Over the years I've come to realize that he was right not to marry me if he didn't love me, but his timing was really lousy. He never should have given me an engagement ring if he had doubts, and he sure shouldn't have waited until a week before the wedding to call it off. I may have been young and immature, but I deserved better than that."

The next morning Elizabeth overslept. She'd intended to get up as soon as Pilar left for work so she could be at the site of the fire by eight o'clock, but she neglected to set her alarm and didn't waken until almost nine.

Jumping out of bed, she pulled on faded jeans, T-shirt and sneakers and drove to the designated parking zone. There was a shuttle bus taking residents up into the hills, and it was getting ready to leave when she got there. She caught it and got off at the street nearest her destination.

For a long time she just stood there looking around her. The stench of burned wood, metal, garbage, and she didn't want to think of what else, was overpowering, and until now she'd been too intent on parking the car and catching the bus to notice her surroundings.

It looked like a war zone; like the pictures of Kuwait after the Persian Gulf War. Everything was leveled—buildings, trees and power lines. Cars that just days before had been the most luxurious, late models were now burned-out hulls littering streets and roads, abandoned in the terrifying rush to outrun the roaring flames and the traffic jams that had blocked escape.

Elizabeth shuddered and started walking. Here and there a brick or stone chimney still stood, and there were a few blackened trunks of valuable old trees pointing skyward, but everything else had been reduced to rubble and ashes.

Wandering in a daze, her gaze darted back and forth trying to take in the destruction that had turned the lush, forestlike setting of her family home into a blackened, barren hell. She missed her street before she realized she had approached it. There were no familiar landmarks, no street signs. She backtracked, but didn't have to wait until she turned the corner to see that her home was gone. All of the homes were gone, the O'Hallorans', the Greens', the Sawyers', even the Tsumuras', and they had only recently replaced their cedar shake roof with tile which was supposed to protect the house from fire.

She was only partially conscious of people along the streets—some crying, others digging through the ashes, some just standing and looking, too shocked and distraught to react. It was like wandering in a nightmare, and when she came to the lot on which her beautiful old home had stood, she looked right through the empty space all the way across the bay to the bridge and the San Francisco peninsula. Where once buildings and trees had obscured the view in places, now all was barren.

The enormity of the disaster, which she'd been keeping at a distance for the past three days, finally hit her and loosened a flood of tears. It was all gone! The pictures, the school yearbooks, the dolls she hadn't been able to bring herself to give away. Her whole childhood was piled in mounds of ash at her feet.

Covering her face with her hands, she sank to a cross-legged position on the dry cement where the garage had been, unable to control the sobs that racked her small frame. How could she tell her unsuspecting parents that they'd lost everything they'd been collecting over the past forty years? Their home, their many valuable pieces of furniture, paintings, and art objects, records of the family history, all things that could never be replaced.

She was wrapped in a ball of misery, unaware of the people coming and going around her. Then someone came over and sat down beside her. Before she could look up, she felt strong arms around her, and a male voice murmured, "I'll let you cry on my shoulder, Elizabeth, if you'll let me cry on yours."

Chapter Four

It was Deny. Elizabeth knew the feel of his embrace, the sound of his voice, even before she raised her head to look at him. His familiar face was only inches from hers, and there were tears in his blue eyes, too.

"Oh, Deny," she sobbed, and put her arms around his neck. "It's so awful." She buried her face in his soft cotton-knit shirt and could feel the muscles of his chest and the rapid beat of his heart.

For a long time they sat there holding each other and cried for their lost homes. In the midst of her own sorrow Elizabeth felt privileged to know that Deny still trusted her enough to cry with her. Like most males he'd always felt that tears were a sign of weakness. When they were still children his dog had been hit by a car in front of the house and killed. He'd remained stoic until they were alone later, but then he'd broken down and sobbed in her arms. Afterward, he'd been ashamed and threatened her with dire consequences if she ever told on him. He needn't have worried, she never had.

When they got their emotions under control and pulled apart to wipe their eyes and blow their noses, Elizabeth was disturbed by the feelings his embrace had aroused. She'd convinced herself that she was over her obsession with Deny, but being held in his arms again felt too much like coming home to a lover.

Even though she'd told him she never wanted to see him again, as long as she lived in Oakland, the odds were that they would run into each other eventually, so she'd long ago made plans for that eventuality. When it happened she'd be polite and friendly but distant. Greet him as she'd greet any acquaintance whom she hadn't seen in a long time, inquire about his life in Washington, answer any questions with short, impersonal statements and then excuse herself and leave.

The scenario had sounded so reasonable when she'd plotted it, but she hadn't counted on such an emotional event bringing them together again. She'd expected to be clearheaded, but her scheme hadn't included a mutual loss and a loving embrace. Now her thoughts were scrambled and her emotions out of control.

This man had hurt her deeply. He'd humiliated her and made her an object of gossip. She'd forgiven him for backing out, once she came to realize that marrying so young would have been a mistake, but she couldn't forget the way he'd gone about it. So why was her heart pounding and her hands trembling?

For several minutes they sat side by side, lost in their individual memories, until finally Deny broke the silence. "Dad says your parents don't know about the fire yet."

Elizabeth shook her head. "No. They're somewhere in the Greek islands on vacation. I . . . I'd give anything if I didn't have to tell them. At least, not until just before time for them to come home..."

Her voice broke. Come home to what? There was no home to come to.

Deny looked at her, and she saw compassion in his expression. "That's not a good idea, Elizabeth. This disaster is international news. It's bound to catch up with them soon. I'm sure you'd rather they heard it from you than on a newscast."

She closed her eyes and sighed. "Yes, of course, but I don't know where they are. They're moving around a lot, but they promised to keep in touch. They usually call every few days when they're on a trip."

She paused, then changed the subject. "Speaking of parents, have you seen your mom this morning? I called the hospital before I left the apartment, and they said she was breathing more easily."

Deny raised his knees and clasped his hands around his shins. "I stopped by to see her on my way here. Dad would have come with me, but I talked him into staying with Mom. All this has been such a shock to him. I'm not sure he's up to seeing..."

He swallowed and didn't continue for a moment. Then he stood and reached his hand down to pull her up. "Look, how about if I help you search through your rubble, then you help me search through mine?"

This was going to be a big job, and she'd be silly not to accept his suggestion. Another hour or so in his company wasn't going to hurt anything. She held out her hand to him. "You're on," she said as he gave her a tug. "I hope you thought to bring heavy gloves. I have mine in my purse."

Deny was wearing a backpack. He took it off and pulled out an assortment of objects—a short-handled shovel, flashlight, clawhammer, as well as gloves. How like him to think ahead and come prepared. And how like her to rush to the scene with very little thought of what she would need once she got there.

He was also more properly dressed than she for the dirty and possibly dangerous work ahead. He'd worn heavy boots to protect his feet and legs from low-lying protruding objects, and a long-sleeved shirt to ward off those at a higher level. Much more appropriate than her soft shoes and T-shirt.

They worked side by side for two hours, sifting through the ashes and digging into the debris on both properties, looking for anything that might have survived the flames, but it was as if a giant blowtorch had hovered over the area, incinerating everything within reach of its heat and flame.

When they were finally certain that nothing had escaped destruction, they gave up and prepared to leave. "Are you up to walking down the hill to the parking lot, or would you rather take the bus?" Deny asked as he stuffed his tools into his backpack.

The idea of getting on a bus in her grimy, sweaty condition was unthinkable. "I'd prefer to walk. I have this...this compulsion to hike through the area. Sort of like paying my last respects at a wake."

She shivered, and Deny put his arm around her shoulders and hugged her to his side. "I know what you mean," he said. "It's a form of mourning, and it's healthier to express it than to bottle it all up."

He released her and strapped on his backpack, then reached for her hand. "Come on, we'll take our time and say goodbye to our past."

They wandered hand in hand through the bleak devastation, speaking little but comfortable in their silence. If Elizabeth could have shut her eyes and blotted out the stifling smell, she could convince herself that it was five years earlier and she and Deny were best friends and sweethearts again.

Everything had been so right then. They'd been happy, content, and their lives stretched ahead of them in one long glorious future together. His hand was rougher now, but still it was familiar. A hand she could cling to, a hand she could trust.

That thought brought her back to the present with a jolt, and she pulled out of his grasp. Good heavens, what was the matter with her? She'd found out the hard way that she could neither cling to Deny nor trust him. She'd better remember that.

He hadn't loved her, even back then. He hadn't wanted to be married to her, and the one thing she knew with absolute certainty was that she no longer wanted to marry him.

She doubted that she'd ever marry anybody. The very thought of a wedding made her physically ill. She hadn't attended one since her own was canceled, although she'd been invited to many. Always she sent a gift along with her regrets, and that went for showers, too. She avoided movies that featured weddings, and if there was one in a television show, she turned the set off.

Deny looked at her questioningly but made no comment about her pulling her hand away from his. Instead he walked quietly along beside her for a few more minutes before he spoke.

"We've got to have a long talk, Elizabeth. I'm sorry you wouldn't answer my calls or read my letters after I left. I wanted so bad to make you understand, to tell you—"

"Oh, I understood," she interrupted. "You made your feelings very clear. We had nothing more to talk about then, and we still don't."

"Yes, we do," he insisted, "but since I've been here, Dad has refused to give me your address, and you're not listed in the phone book."

Elizabeth was uneasy. She didn't want to quarrel with him, but neither did she intend to let him break through her reserve.

"Aidan doesn't know my address, and you're right, I'm not listed in the phone book," she said, not volunteering the information that their phone was listed under Pilar's name.

Once more they walked in silence until he spoke again and startled her. "Now that I've found you I'm determined that we'll finally have that talk. Will you have lunch with me today?"

He must have seen her step falter, because he hurried on. "After all, we were best friends for twenty years, and I've missed you. I know I don't deserve your friendship anymore, but can't we at least be acquaintances for an hour or so?"

Elizabeth was surprised by the invitation, and appalled at how much she wanted to accept. Instinctively she knew that it was a dangerous move to consider. She was still tingling from the embrace they'd shared earlier. They'd been too close for too long a time for her to be able to shut him out and forget him. It hadn't happened in over three years. And it wasn't likely to happen in the foreseeable future unless....

She had to admit that he was right about so much being left unsaid between them when they'd parted with such a wrench. Maybe the wounds would heal more easily if they did sit down together and try to resolve the lingering pain they'd caused each other. On the other hand they could be opening themselves up for even more anguish, and she knew she couldn't stand that.

Elizabeth realized that she was cornered. Since she was too proud to let him know just how deeply he'd hurt her, she couldn't banish him entirely. Besides, he'd only be around for a few days, so what harm could having one meal together do?

"Elizabeth?" Deny looked anxious. "Please. Just for old times' sake if nothing else?"

She might as well give in. Then maybe he'd leave her alone. "All right, if it's that important to you," she said in her best offhanded manner, "but I can't stay long. I have to see the insurance adjuster this afternoon."

He looked relieved, and she wondered why it was so important to him. Could it be that his parents were pressuring him to make up with her? She knew Uncle Aidan and Aunt Maggie both felt bad about the way Deny had broken their engagement.

Well, if that was it, they could forget it. She wasn't going to let either set of parents coerce her into anything again. She made her own decisions now.

"Good," he said, and looked at his watch. "How about meeting me at Spenger's in an hour? That will give us time to shower and change."

Spenger's Fish Grotto was a longtime popular restaurant in Berkeley just across the freeway from Oakland. "Okay, I'll meet you there at one," she said, and wondered if she was making a grave error in judgment.

Well, if she was, it wouldn't be the first time.

Elizabeth drove into Spenger's jammed parking lot with five minutes to spare, but still Deny was there, waiting for her just inside the entrance of the warehouselike building situated under the freeway.

"You're early," she accused as he stepped out of the shadows of the dimly lit interior.

He must have rushed to clean up and look so bandbox fresh in his knife-creased gray slacks and navy blue blazer. She noticed that he was wearing his black hair shorter on the sides and back now, but it still curled on top.

"Yes," he admitted. "I didn't want to give you an excuse to leave if I wasn't here when you arrived."

He took her arm and they followed the hostess around the plain wooden tables and chairs in the rustic dining room until she seated them at the only empty table in a corner at the back. There was a nautical atmosphere about the restaurant, with decorative anchors, mastheads, seashells and netting scattered throughout. Sort of like eating in the mess hall of a ship, but with an outstanding seafood menu.

After they gave their orders to the waitress, Elizabeth asked Deny if his job in Washington had been as fulfilling as he'd expected it would be.

"If you mean has it been a satisfactory substitute for you the answer is no. It hasn't and never will be."

His unexpected comment sent prickles down her spine. "That's not what I meant!" she said heatedly.

"Maybe not," he replied, "but that's my answer. Nearly three and a half years ago I made a choice between marrying you and taking that job, and I made the wrong decision. That's what I was trying to tell you with my letters and phone calls, but you wouldn't give me a chance."

Elizabeth blinked with surprise. Now what was he up to? "I'm sorry you feel that way," she said carefully, "because, although I couldn't see it at the time, I know now that you were right. If you think you've broken my heart and need to make amends, forget it. It didn't take me long to realize that you did me a favor by calling off the wedding, so if you're feeling guilty, don't."

Elizabeth knew she wasn't being truthful. He *had* broken her heart, and for a long time the pain had been cutting and raw. It had been well over a year before she'd stopped grieving and acknowledged the fact that she liked being independent of both Deny and her parents. She had come to feel that her career in nursing, where she could be of real service to suffering humanity, was, in a way, as rewarding as a husband and family would have been.

Maybe someday she could have all three, but not with Denis O'Halloran.

Before he could react to her comments, the waitress arrived with their food, and set the shrimp salad in front of Elizabeth and the lobster thermidor in front of Deny. A basket of San Francisco sourdough bread accompanied the food, and the waitress poured coffee for them from a carafe then left it on the table.

For a time they were distracted by the business of buttering their bread and adding cream to their coffee, but after they'd taken the first few bites Deny cleared his throat and looked across the table at Elizabeth.

"What I feel isn't guilt so much as remorse," he said, returning to their interrupted conversation. "I never meant to hurt you the way I did. You were my sweetheart, my best friend in all the world, and I didn't want to lose you. I only wanted to give us a little time away from each other to make sure we were ready for the commitment of marriage."

She took a swallow of ice water before she answered. "I'm sorry, Deny, but I don't believe you."

He frowned and opened his mouth to protest as she hurried on. "Oh, I know you didn't intend to hurt me, but you were so anxious to get out of marrying me that you panicked and said whatever was necessary to get me to call it off."

"That's not true—"

"Oh, for God's sake, don't deny it," she said, fighting to keep her voice steady. "You didn't have any intention of going through with the wedding. You'd made arrangements to fly to Washington the following day before you even talked to me, and that was a week before the scheduled ceremony. I'm not interested in hearing about your feelings, because you've lied to me quite consistently about them.''

He glared at her. "Elizabeth, I've never lied to you!"

She glared back. "If you believe that then you're lying to yourself. You told me you loved me, asked me to marry you, said you wanted to spend your life with me, when all the while you were simply mouthing what our parents wanted you to say."

Again he started to speak, but she held up her hand. "No, hear me out. I've had a lot of time to think about this. You caved in to parental pressure and gave me an engagement ring that last Christmas, but as the time grew nearer for the wedding you knew it wasn't what you wanted."

Her voice broke and she took a deep breath before plunging along. "I realize now that I was self-centered and shallow. I was a generation behind the times. My greatest ambition was to be like my mother, with a husband to take care of me and children who were bright and beautiful extensions of myself."

He shook his head vigorously and tried to interrupt, but she hurried on. "You were no doubt thoroughly sick of my childishness, but you had no right to let me forge ahead happily planning any wedding, big or small, when you knew you didn't want me for a wife."

His features twisted in an expression of disbelief and denial. "Oh, sweetheart," he groaned. "You don't know me at all."

"You're right, I don't," she said hollowly. "I used to think I knew everything about you, but you stripped me of that illusion. It seems that the boy I grew up with and loved so dearly was a phantom of my imagination. I was a silly little girl who lived in a dreamworld that my parents and my upbringing perpetuated. You blew apart that fantasy and shoved me into the world of reality. It was painful, but I survived to be grateful that you did it. My life is so much more meaningful now."

He shook his head, but just then the waitress appeared to clear the table and bring their desserts. Elizabeth eyed the chocolate mousse piled high with whipped cream, and wondered why she'd thought she could eat that after the big salad.

Deny looked at his cherry pie à la mode, but picked up his cup of coffee instead of a fork. He seemed uneasy as he took a swallow then put the cup down. "Elizabeth," he said hesitantly. "Has there been . . . that is . . . is there someone special in your life now?"

She hadn't expected him to change the subject, and wasn't sure she understood his question. "What do you mean by someone special?"

Again he picked up his cup and clasped both hands around it. "I mean a man," he said sharply. "Do you have a man in your life?"

Elizabeth stared at him, unable to believe he'd actually asked that question.

"That's really none of your business, Deny," she said coolly, "but since you asked I'll tell you. There's been no room in my life for a man, special or otherwise. When I was in school I studied every minute that I wasn't in classes or actually working in the hospital. Since I got my R.N. I've been putting in some long days in the trauma center. Frankly, after ten or twelve hours of patching people up who are brought in after automobile accidents, fires, shootings, stabbings, and botched suicide attempts, I don't have much time or energy for dates."

It seemed to her that he looked almost pleased, but why would it matter to him one way or the other?

"Now it's your turn," she said. "Is there a special woman in your life?"

Immediately she was sorry she'd asked. If there was, she didn't want to know it, but he shook his head. "No. My time's been limited, too. I've been attending night school to get my master's degree. Besides, I've never found a woman who measures up to you."

Elizabeth was stunned at the wave of relief that last admission evoked, and she quickly replaced it with anger as she pushed back her chair and stood. "Oh, stop it, Deny." Her tone was low. "I told you, you don't owe me anything. I'm not the same willful brat you grew up with. I know now that I'd never have been happy as a compliant little housewife having babies every other year and relying on a man to make me a whole person."

She picked up her purse and slung it over her shoulder. "Thank you for the lunch, and have a good trip back to D.C."

Hospital nurses had to work a long time before accumulating enough seniority to get weekends off, and the following day, Thursday, was supposed to be Elizabeth's second free day that week. But at five in the morning she was wakened by a call asking if she could substitute for a nurse who was ill. She groaned but agreed and even managed to arrive early enough to look in on Maggie before reporting to the floor. Since it was so early she was pretty sure she wouldn't run into Deny.

A glance at Maggie's chart told her that the cautious optimism of the report the day before had been premature. Her temperature was up again and her breathing was labored. Elizabeth quietly walked across the floor to the cubicle where Deny's mother lay hooked up to various tubes and needles. Her graying hair was disheveled, and she looked flushed and feverish.

Her eyes were closed but she moved restlessly, and when Elizabeth touched her hand, her lids fluttered open. "Elizabeth," she said in little more than a whisper as her own hand turned to clasp the one holding it.

"Good morning, Aunt Maggie." She forced a smile. "Is there anything I can do for you?"

"I . . . I'd like some water."

"Of course." Elizabeth picked up the glass containing a bent straw and encouraged her patient to sip.

"Denis says that both our houses are gone," Maggie said sadly as she waved the glass away.

Elizabeth knew that Deny wouldn't have volunteered that information to his mother while she was so ill, but she also knew that Maggie wouldn't have been put off with evasions.

"Yes, they are," she confirmed, "but try to look on the brighter side. The houses were fully insured. Our two families are better off than those who were underinsured, or, worse, suffered major burns or deaths."

Maggie's lips trembled, and tears rolled down her face. "I know, but still it's hard. . . ."

Elizabeth stroked the grieving woman's hair. "Of course it is, but we're all survivors, Aunt Maggie. We'll learn to accept our losses and start over."

Maggie sighed. "That's easier to do when you're young. . . ." She seemed to cut off that line of thought and abruptly changed the subject. "Deny also says you two had lunch together yesterday. Did you have a nice time?"

Her tone had brightened, and Elizabeth wasn't going to dim it by telling her they'd quarreled. Maggie needed all the hope she could get right now.

"Yes, very nice," she said lightly. "We had a long talk and caught up on what has been going on in each other's lives during the past three years."

She glanced at her watch, anxious to escape before Maggie pinned her down with difficult questions. "Oh dear, I'll be late for work if I don't hurry."

She squeezed Maggie's hand. "You concentrate on getting well, and let the rest of us handle the details involving the fire. I'll be back up later to check on you again."

Elizabeth worked an extra two hours that afternoon and was later than usual getting home. Pilar was just taking a baking dish of beef enchiladas out of the oven, and the spicy aroma reminded her that she was hungry.

"Oh, good, you're just in time to eat with me," Pilar said as she set the dish on a hot pad on the table, then hurried to put out another place setting. "I assume you got stuck at the hospital past quitting time?"

Elizabeth put her purse on the breakfast bar and sat down at the table. "Yeah, there was a pileup on the freeway, and they brought the casualties to us. I guess you'd already left when they arrived. No one was seriously injured, but it took a while to patch them up and admit the ones who needed further care."

Pilar took a fresh tossed salad out of the refrigerator and put it on the table, then sat down, too.

For a few minutes they were busy dishing up their food, but as soon as Pilar had swallowed her first bite of enchilada and pronounced it edible, she looked at Elizabeth and grinned. "So, how are your Aunt Maggie and Uncle Aidan today?"

Elizabeth grinned back. She knew what her friend was fishing for, but instead of telling her what she wanted to know, she answered the question. "Maggie is still pretty sick, but she seemed to be breathing a little easier when I saw her before I left. Aidan's burns are painful, but he won't admit it, and he refuses to stay home and rest.''

"But his home was destroyed," Pilar pointed out. "Where is he staying?"

"With his son Finley and family in the Berkeley Hills, but Deny is registered at a hotel in town near the hospital. Aidan could rest there at intervals during the day, but he won't leave Maggie.''

"And Deny?" The words nearly burst from Pilar. "Did you see him today?"

Elizabeth laughed. Naturally her audacious apartment mate knew about Elizabeth's lunch with Deny yesterday, and she was dying to know what had happened today.

"Down, girl," Elizabeth teased. "I didn't see him. I understand he was at the hospital part of the day, but according to his brothers, he went to San Francisco this afternoon to see his sister, Rosalie, and her family. She's just had a new baby, and hasn't been over to see her mother yet.''

Half an hour later they'd finished eating, and Elizabeth was preparing to do the dishes while Pilar dressed to go to a movie with one of the dark, handsome Latin men she dated. Pilar was fiercely proud of her Mexican roots and seldom went out with Anglo men.

Elizabeth smiled as she remembered her roommate's explanation. *It's just as easy to fall in love with a Latino as an Anglo man, and I want my children to have one heritage only—mine.*

A jangle of discordant bells split the air, and it took Elizabeth a moment to figure out that it was both the telephone and the door. "You get the door," she called to Pilar, "and I'll answer the phone."

She knew by the rather hollow sound of the slight crackle on the line that it was an overseas call even before her mother's voice answered her greeting. "Hello, Elizabeth, this is Mother. How are you?"

Elizabeth's stomach knotted and her hand tightened on the receiver. Her reprieve was over. She was going to have to tell her parents about the fire, but how could she do it without giving them a dangerous shock? Thank God, although her mom, Kathleen, was sixty-five and her dad, Connor, sixty-eight, they were both strong and healthy with no sign of heart disease.

"I'm fine, Mom," she answered. "Where are you?"

"We're back in Athens, and are leaving tomorrow for Egypt. We've been having the most marvelous time. The Greek Islands are fascinating and..."

She babbled on, excitedly telling her daughter about the digs they'd been on, the treasures they'd seen unearthed, and the extraordinary people they'd met. They'd been roughing it a bit on the digs, but the suite they had in Athens right now was absolutely lovely, her mother told her. While her mother talked, Elizabeth murmured an appropriate comment here and there as she tried desperately to find the words she needed to deliver the bad news and at the same time cushion the blow.

Finally, the voice at the other end stopped and she knew time had run out. She had to say something.

Taking a deep breath, she sat down on one of the breakfast bar stools and tried to gather her courage. "Uh...I'm glad you're having so much fun," she stammered. "Mother, what time is it there?"

"Why, it's..." Kathleen paused for a moment. "I'm not sure. I'm not wearing my watch, but it's very early morning. Still dark. We tried to get you yesterday afternoon and evening, since Thursday is usually your day off, but no one answered the phone. It is Thursday in California, isn't it?"

"Yes, Mom, it is, but I worked today. We've been awfully busy at the hospital. Um . . . is Dad there?"

"He just went into the bedroom to pick up the extension," her mother replied.

Then Connor's voice came on the line. "Hello, honey."

"Oh, hi, Dad," she said, trying to match his cheerful tone. She took a deep breath. They had to know, she reminded herself. She had to tell them.

"Elizabeth, is something wrong?" her father said, and she could hear the quick change from gaiety to concern in his voice.

She should have known she couldn't hide anything from her quick-witted father. Not even from across the American continent, the Atlantic Ocean and most of Europe.

She took another deep breath and plunged ahead. "Yes, Daddy, Mom, I'm sorry to say there is."

She closed her eyes and told them the heartbreaking news. "Last Sunday a fire started in the hills. It turned into a holocaust and raced through the East Bay hills, destroying everything in its path!"

Chapter Five

Elizabeth heard both parents gasp, but it was her father who recovered enough to ask the inevitable question first. "Our house...?"

"Yes." It was more of a choking sound than an answer, but they understood.

For a moment there was only stunned silence, then she heard Kathleen's anguished cry and Connor's muttered, "Oh, my God!"

"I'm so—" Elizabeth's throat convulsed and she tried again. "I'm so sorry. It happened so fast. By the time I heard about it, the blaze was out of control, and the main concern was getting the people out. The whole area was sealed off. There was no way I could get up there to try to save at least some of our things."

Kathleen sobbed, and Connor's voice was gravelly with shock. "Well, thank the Lord for that," he said. "Losing the house is bad enough, but if we'd lost you..." She could almost hear him shudder.

"I'm all right," she assured them, "but the last I heard there were nineteen dead, thousands left homeless, and nearly one billion dollars in damages. The toll will undoubtedly be higher. They're still searching—"

"Aidan and Maggie!" Connor interrupted. "Are they...?"

"They were taken out by helicoptor, but they were both brought to the hospital. Aidan with first- and second-degree burns and Maggie with emphysema complicated by smoke inhalation. Aidan was released Monday, but Maggie's still there. Their house is gone, too."

Again there was silence except for Kathleen's keening.

Finally Connor spoke again. "Look, honey, I'm going to ring off now. We need a little time to absorb...we'll call back in half an hour or so."

Elizabeth was relieved. She needed time, too, to deal with all she had to tell them. "All right, Dad, but don't make any decisions until we talk again, okay."

She hung up and spent the next forty minutes organizing her thoughts and jotting down questions she wanted to ask and facts that it was important they know. When they called back, they were both a little more in control, and she started at the beginning and gave them a full account of the tragedy to date.

At intervals they stopped her to ask a question or make a comment, but mostly they let her tell it in her own way. Her mother sobbed unceasingly, and Elizabeth could hear her father's frequent comforting murmurs.

"I know you can't think of anything right now but the staggering loss you've suffered," she said in conclusion as she swiped with the back of her hand at the tears streaming down her cheeks, "but later you'll realize that, compared to many, we were fortunate. We lost things, but none of the Kellys or the O'Hallorans were seriously injured or killed."

She pressed her lips together to stop them from trembling and waited for one of her parents to comment.

Again it was Connor who spoke. "Yes, you're right, of course," he said shakily. "But it's still a terrible blow. I'm sorry you couldn't reach us earlier, but we'll catch the first flight out—"

"No, Dad, please don't do that," Elizabeth interrupted. "I want you to continue your vacation. Go on to Egypt as you'd planned—"

"Don't be silly, girl," he snapped. "Of course we're coming home. I have to make arrangements for—"

"Daddy, listen to me!" Elizabeth almost shouted into the phone. "I've done all that can be done right now. I've talked with the insurance people and the lawyers, and they're handling everything."

"But I need to be there to sign papers, and inventory our losses—"

"That's all being taken care of. The law firm has a limited power of attorney for you, remember? And, Dad, I'm sorry, but there's no need for an inventory. You lost everything."

Her mother's voice rose in a cry of grief that started Elizabeth's tears flowing again, but she had to make them understand that it was best if they got used to the fact of this catastrophe before they saw the devastation.

She could hear Connor trying to comfort Kathleen, and she waited until her mother excused herself to go to the bathroom and try to compose herself before she spoke again. "Dad, is Mom all right? Maybe you should have the hotel call a doctor."

"Yes, I'll do that," he assured her. "He can at least give her a sedative. This has been a dreadful shock."

"I know," she said, then lowered her voice. "Would you please hang up the other phone? I want to talk to you in private."

When he indicated that he'd done as she asked, she got right to the point. "I haven't told you everything," she said hesitantly. "Aunt Maggie is in intensive care, and Emily Carpenter was one of those killed. Also, Jim Oswald was burned on over eighty percent of his body and isn't expected to live."

The last two people she mentioned had been longtime friends, and fairly close neighbors.

"Oh, dear Lord," Connor breathed. He sounded as if he'd been hit in the stomach.

"I'm so sorry. I hadn't wanted to tell you that until later, but you need to understand why I don't want you to bring Mother back here until she's had a chance to get used to the scope of this fire storm. You can't even imagine what it looks like up there. I've saved the newspapers, and I'll send them to you, but at least give me time to find you a condominium so you'll have a place to come home to."

There was another pause as her father fought to recover from this latest blow. "I suppose you're right," he finally said. "I'd like to spare your mother the final horror of actually seeing the ruins until she's better able to deal with it. Are you sure you can handle everything?"

Elizabeth breathed a sigh of relief. "Yes, Dad, just keep me posted as to your current address and phone number."

Her mother came out of the bathroom and Elizabeth talked for several more minutes with both parents. She patiently answered their questions and gave them all the information she could. "I'm going to hang up now," she said at last, "but I have the name and number of the hotel where you'll be staying in Cairo. I'll call you there in approximately..." she looked at her watch and did some figuring in her head "... twenty-seven hours."

"All right, dear," her mother said in a voice that still trembled, "but you must promise to contact us immediately if Maggie..." Her voice broke and she sobbed. "If Maggie gets worse tell ... tell her and Aidan that we'll come immediately."

"Of course I will, Mother," Elizabeth assured her, and this time the tears that broke through were tears of happiness that the long feud between the families was over.

Elizabeth left for the hospital earlier than usual the following morning so she'd have time to check on Maggie and, if she was awake, deliver Kathleen and Connor's message of condolence and concern.

After changing into her green scrubs, she hurried up to the second floor, where a review of the patient's chart with the head nurse on duty was not encouraging. Maggie's temperature had escalated rather than subsided as it should with the medication she was getting, and she'd had episodes of mental confusion.

For the first time Elizabeth felt tendrils of real fear. Maggie should be getting better, but she wasn't! With the advent of antibiotics, pneumonia was seldom the life-threatening illness it had once been, but with the complications of emphysema and smoke inhalation and the fact that she was over sixty, the prognosis could still be grim.

Elizabeth walked over to the bed, and Maggie opened her eyes. "Kathleen?" she said, looking at Elizabeth but apparently seeing her mother.

Elizabeth picked up the small, hot hand that lay on top of the lightweight blanket and held it between both of hers. "No, Aunt Maggie, it's Elizabeth. Mom's in Greece, remember?"

Maggie blinked, and her eyes focused a little more accurately. "Oh, yes. I don't know what's the matter with me. Kathleen wouldn't be visiting me even if she were in town." She sounded sad.

"Yes, she would," Elizabeth assured her. "I talked to Dad and Mom last night, and they were prepared to catch the first flight out in order to come back and be with you. In fact, I had to insist that they not come, but if you want them here all I have to do is phone and tell them."

Maggie rolled her head back and forth on the pillow. "No, don't do that. They probably wouldn't be permitted to visit me in here anyway."

A tiny smile tipped the corners of her mouth. "I'm glad they wanted to come, though."

Elizabeth squeezed the hand she held. "Mother gave me strict instructions to call anytime day or night if you need her."

Maggie didn't answer. She'd lapsed into sleep with the tiny smile still on her lips. Carefully Elizabeth released her hand and walked away.

She didn't like this new turn in Maggie's condition. She apparently wasn't responding to the medication. Her overall health was good, so why wasn't her body able to throw off the infection?

Elizabeth was debating in her mind on whether or not it would be advisable to question Maggie's doctor when she collided with Deny in the hall. His arms circled her waist, and she clutched at his shoulders as they sought to steady themselves.

"Deny!" she exclaimed in surprise. "I'm sorry. I wasn't watching where I was going." She pushed herself back, but his arms tightened. "What are you doing here so early?"

He pulled her closer and she relaxed in his embrace. He'd grown and filled out in the years since they'd last seen each other. He'd still been something of a boy then, now it was a man who held her. Without willing them to, her hands slid over his shoulders and crossed behind his neck, and she could feel his powerful muscles under his thin shirt.

"I couldn't sleep," he said, "so I decided to come over and check on Mom. She looked so flushed and uncomfortable when I left last night. She's not doing well, is she?" It was more a statement, than a question.

"Not as well as we'd hoped," she murmured against his chest. "Have you talked to her doctor?"

He caressed the top of her head with his chin. "The whole family ganged up on him last night when he came to see her. He says she has a particularly virulent type of pneumonia and it's resisting the usual antibiotics. Who is that man anyway? Why can't our family doctor take care of her?"

She could sympathize with his concern but tried to lessen his fear. "He's the best thoracic specialist in the Bay Area," she assured him. "Her own doctor called him in and is also checking on her daily. From what I've read on her chart they seem to be doing all they can, but if you'd like another opinion...maybe an infectious disease specialist...?"

"No," he said with a sigh. "Not yet, but if she gets any worse..."

He didn't finish the sentence but hugged her as if drawing strength from their physical contact. "How is she this morning?"

"About the same as last night." Elizabeth didn't tell him Maggie had mistaken her for her mother, but she did tell him about her conversation with her own parents. "At least one good thing has come out of this," she concluded. "The long estrangement between our families is over. Believe me, I never wanted our breakup to cause such a rift between them."

"It wasn't your fault," he murmured, "it was mine. In my clumsy way of handling it, I messed up everybody's lives. I couldn't be happier that they're finally healing the rift. Now if only we..."

He didn't continue but just held her close.

Elizabeth was vaguely aware of people passing them there in the hall, but the steady beat of Deny's heart beneath her cheek, and the solid length of his body pressed against hers, so enthralled her that she forgot where she was and what she was supposed to be doing.

She wasn't sure how long they stood there wrapped in each other's arms before Deny spoke and broke the spell. "Do you have time for a cup of coffee with me?"

She returned to reality with a start and pulled away to look at her watch. "Oh my, I'm going to have to hurry or I'll be late. Sorry..."

The elevator bell rang just then, and she hurried down the hall to catch it. It wasn't until she was inside and slumped against the wall that she realized she felt light-headed and her knees were trembling. So much for her efforts to relegate Denis O'Halloran to the role of casual friend!

Maggie's condition continued to hover between "fair" and "guarded" as Elizabeth found out from numerous calls to ICU during the day. She didn't get worse, but neither was she any better, and the mounting worry that nagged at Elizabeth also made it difficult to concentrate on her own patients.

At the end of her shift she quickly changed into her black slacks and black-and-white pullover shirt and hurried upstairs. Aidan was sitting beside Maggie's bed, and a reading of the chart told Elizabeth that there was still no change.

She walked across to the cubicle and put her hand on Aidan's shoulder. He looked up at her, and the anxious expression on his white face and the fear that darkened his turquoise eyes told her, better than words, of his anguish. He'd aged considerably in the past few days, and she could see that he was exhausted.

"Uncle Aidan," she said quietly, "you're going to be ill if you don't get some rest. Why don't you let Deny take you to his hotel so you can lie down for a while?"

She could feel the tension in his slumped shoulder. "Not until her temperature goes down and she can breathe easier," he said firmly. "She needs me."

"Of course she does," Elizabeth agreed, "but you won't be any good to her if you collapse and have to be admitted to the hospital, too. You have serious burns, and it's time you started taking care of yourself. Let's go out to the waiting room and talk to the boys. Are they all here?"

"The boys," was the way Aidan and Maggie always referred to their four sons even now that they were adults.

"Yes, they're here," he said, and Elizabeth noticed that he didn't refuse to talk with them about her suggestion.

Aidan's sons greeted their father and Elizabeth when they entered the waiting room, and, in the usual O'Halloran manner, the oldest son, Seamus, held out his arms and hugged her when she went to him. "Little Lizzie," he said, using his favorite nickname for her, "Jill and I seem to have just missed you ever since we got here. How are you?"

He held her away from him as they looked each other over. Seamus was fourteen years older than Deny, which would make him forty-one, Elizabeth calculated. His hairline had receded slightly, and he'd put on weight since she last saw him, but the O'Halloran trademark-blue eyes still sparkled, and his grin was as infectious as she remembered it.

"You've grown up to be a beautiful woman," he observed.

She felt herself blush. "Thank you," she said demurely. "You're looking great, too. Is Jill here?"

She glanced around the room but saw none of the O'Halloran women, although her gaze roamed over Finley and Glendon before meshing with Deny's.

"No," Seamus answered. "She and Lucy went back to Finley's to see about the kids." He looked at his father. "How's Mom?"

Aidan shook his head. "About the same. She's sleeping."

"And that's what Uncle Aidan should be doing," Elizabeth said to the four brothers. "He's exhausted and in pain, and I'm trying to convince him to go to Deny's hotel room and lie down. I hope you can help me. He really needs to rest more."

All four of the "boys" agreed with her and took turns arguing with their father until they finally wore him down and he reluctantly capitulated. "All right, I'm obviously not going to have any peace until I do. But you've got to promise to bring me back when I say so."

Elizabeth was quite certain he'd fall asleep as soon as he stretched out on a bed, and she nodded at Deny.

"I learned long ago not to argue with you," Deny told his father, "but we're going to take Elizabeth along to make sure you get some rest. She always could wrap you around her little finger." He looked at her and winked.

"Oh, but I—" she started to say, but Deny interrupted.

"I have a suite so he'll have plenty of privacy and quiet..." Deny paused and looked uncertain. "That is, unless you have other plans for the evening."

She didn't, but neither did she want to be alone in a hotel room with him. Not that she was afraid he'd force his attentions on her, but she didn't like the way her traitorous body reacted to his nearness. She remembered all too well the thrill of his lips moving on hers, his thigh brushing against hers, and the way his fingers could bring her nipples to hard, throbbing peaks with their gentle manipulations.

A flush of heat forced her attention back to the present, and she turned her face away, hoping he hadn't seen her blush.

"I...no, I haven't any plans," she heard herself say, and groaned inwardly.

You idiot! You're playing with fire, and it can burn you just as deeply as the one that raced through the hills!

"Good, then we'd better be on our way," Deny said, and turned to his brothers. "Tell Lucy not to wait dinner for us. We'll get something to eat at the hotel before we come back."

Elizabeth had been secluded in the hospital all day and didn't realize until she stepped outside with Deny and Aidan that the morning drizzle had turned into a steady afternoon rain. None of them had umbrellas, and the two men took off in one direction and Elizabeth in another as they sprinted toward their cars.

She followed Deny to the hotel and turned her car over to the valet for parking. Deny's suite consisted of two separate rooms and a short connecting hallway at the front with a door at each end. The room on the right was furnished as a bedroom, and the one on the left as a living room with a fully stocked bar in one corner.

Aidan argued but Deny finally got him to loosen or remove clothing that was uncomfortable and crawl into bed.

"I don't intend to sleep, just rest for a short time," he grumbled as he pulled the top sheet and blanket over himself.

"Sure, Dad, but the air conditioning in here is pretty powerful, and you don't want to get chilled," Deny said as

Elizabeth closed the heavy drapes across the picture window as unobtrusively as possible so he wouldn't object to that, too.

While Deny was gently urging his father into bed, she'd noticed that he looked almost as haggard as Aidan. When they finally closed the bedroom door behind them and went into the living room, he seated her on one end of the long, chocolate-colored velour couch, then slumped down beside her and sighed.

"This has been a long day," he said, and rubbed his hands over his face.

A powerful urge to reach out to him, to settle his head on her shoulder and stroke her fingers through his hair swept over her. It took all her willpower to resist. Instead, she clenched her hands in her lap and took a deep breath. "Yes, it has," she agreed. "You've been at the hospital since shortly after six this morning, and you said you hadn't been able to sleep before that. You need a nap as badly as Aidan does, and I'm going to leave now so you can take one."

She started to get up, but he caught her hand and pulled her back down. "No. Stay. You've been on your feet all day. Stay and take a nap with me."

The idea appealed to her so strongly that she spoke more harshly than she'd intended. "I can't do that. There's only room for you on this couch, and, besides, I don't take naps with men."

He still held her hand, and she couldn't seem to bring herself to pull it away. "I'm glad to hear that," he said gently, "but I'm not just any man. I'm the one you grew up with. Remember when we were little we used to go skinny-dipping in the pool until our parents caught us and made us stop?"

Again she felt the warm color rise to her face. She was also remembering other times they'd gone skinny-dipping when they weren't so young. That memory brought with it vivid pictures of his magnificently tanned and muscular body, not yet a man but certainly not a boy.

She knew he was remembering it, too, and her blush deepened. "It's not at all gentlemanly of you to mention that," she snapped.

Deny said nothing but his grin was devilish. Elizabeth stood and started for the door, but he followed and caught her around the waist.

"I'm sorry, sweetheart, I didn't mean to embarrass you." His tone was properly contrite. "Come, I want to show you something."

He walked her over to one wall and opened a door that was nearly hidden by the pattern of the rich paneling. He reached in and pulled down a queen-size wall bed all made up and ready to use. It took up a good share of the middle of the room.

"This bed is plenty big enough for both of us to stretch out on," he pointed out, "and I promise to stay on my own side and keep my hands to myself."

Elizabeth's eyes widened as she struggled with conflicting emotions. After what he'd done to her she could never trust him again, but still the temptation to curl up with him on that flowered quilt was almost impossible to resist.

"I...I can't lie on the bed with you," she said, and wished her tone had come through stronger and more emphatic.

"Why not?" He shrugged. "It wouldn't be the first time. According to our mothers, we sometimes shared a crib."

"That's not the same and you know it." She didn't care for his teasing.

"I agree," he said easily, "but how about all those lazy summer days when we used to lie side by side on the lawn and talk about what we wanted to be when we grew up. As I remember, you wanted to be a nurse even then."

The vision of those peaceful long-ago interludes made her smile. "Yes, I did." Her voice was soft with memories. "Although I went through one period of hankering for fame and fortune as a movie star."

Deny chuckled. "Hey, I remember that. You wanted to star as Scarlett in a remake of *Gone With the Wind*, and went around all the time practicing your Southern accent. If I'm not mistaken, that was about the time I was in training to be a world-famous spy."

Elizabeth laughed. "Yeah, just after you gave up plans to be a magician, and before you decided to become the next Wilt Chamberlain of basketball."

They both laughed, but then, as if on cue, the laughter stopped. Deny reached out and stroked her hair away from her cheek sending shivers down her spine. "Stay with me, honey. I need you. If you'd rather not share the bed, then I'll take the couch. I just want to know that you're close by."

I need you. Those words, coupled with the anxiety in his eyes and the feel of his fingers gently caressing her cheek almost melted her resolve, and she cast around desperately for the many reasons why she couldn't allow that.

Sure he needed her now. He didn't have a wife to help him bear the anguish of his mother's illness and the loss of his family home, and good old Liz could always be counted on to come through in a pinch. After all, he could throw her over again once he was through with her.

She closed her eyes and swayed slightly as bitterness rocked her, but Deny's voice steadied her. "Elizabeth. Honey, did I say something wrong? I didn't mean . . ."

She shook her head, dislodging his hand, then opened her eyes and looked at him. She wasn't going to let that ugly emotion tear her apart again. She'd fought too long and too hard to overcome it after the wedding was canceled.

"No, you didn't say anything wrong," she assured him. "It's just that . . . well, sometimes memories can be awfully painful. I'm sorry, I wish I could accommodate you, but I really have to be going—"

"I'm not asking to be *accommodated*." His tone was tight with anger. "Forgive me, I won't bother you again." He moved away from her and walked over to look out the window at the ships and cabin cruisers that plied the rough waters of the bay.

Oh, damn! Now she'd hurt and angered him, and that was never what she'd intended. He had about all the torment he could handle without her adding to it. What harm could it do to lie down with him and take a nap? It's not as if she'd never lain next to him before. After all, they'd been engaged to be married at one time.

She walked over to stand beside him, then put her hand on his arm. "I'm sorry," she said quietly. "I don't know why everything we say to each other seems to come out wrong. I didn't mean to sound so cold and accusing. I . . . I guess I haven't come to terms with all the resentment and bitterness. . . ."

He turned and put his arms around her. "Don't ever apologize to me, Elizabeth. None of this is your fault. You're entitled to be bitter and resentful of me and what I did to you. I had no right to ask you to sleep with me, even though I really did mean sleep."

He hugged her close, then abruptly released her and stepped back. "You'd better run along now. You probably have a lot of things to do when you get home. Thank you for helping get Dad to come over here and rest for a while."

He was giving her a clear out. She could leave with his blessing and not have to feel guilty. So why didn't she go, instead of just standing there, looking at him as if she couldn't tear her gaze away from the lines of exhaustion on his face and the yearning that darkened his eyes?

No. She wasn't going to give in to this dangerous lure. It was too foolhardy.

Turning, she started toward the door and made it half-way across the room before she stopped and turned back. He still stood there watching her.

She couldn't leave him. Not now when he really did need her. She held out her hand. "Deny." Her tone was low and her lips quivered. "I'd like to stay if you still want me to."

His gaze never left hers. "I still want you to," he said huskily, and walked toward her.

He took her hand and brought it to his mouth. "Thank you," he murmured, then kissed her palm and held it against his cheek. "Which side of the bed do you want, right or left?"

"The side next to the window if you don't mind," she said, then quickly removed her hand from his face when she noticed that she was caressing him with her fingers.

He took her hand again and led her back to the bed, seated her on the side, then squatted down in front of her. Before she realized what he was going to do, he took one of her feet, put it on his thigh and started to untie her canvas shoe.

"I can do that myself," she said, and tried to pull her foot away, but his hand tightened around her ankle.

"No need, I've got it," he murmured, and slid the sneaker off. Setting it on the floor, he massaged her stock-inged foot between his talented hands.

The sensuous manipulation was so relaxing that she didn't even think to protest but sighed with contentment. "Oh, that feels so good," she moaned. "My feet get tired after being on them all day."

"Of course they do," he said sympathetically as he placed her foot back on his leg, then picked up her other foot and put it on his other thigh to start the process over again.

Elizabeth hadn't realized before how soothing the muscles in the feet could relax the whole body, but as his strong hands stroked and pressed and stretched the aching sinews and tendons, within minutes the tension that had been tormenting her was gone. She felt like a rag doll about to flop over to one side, but before she could, Deny picked up her feet and twisted her around so he could stretch her legs out in front of her on the bed.

"Now, lie down," he said. "Do you need a blanket . . . ?"

She did as he suggested, and sighed as her tired back and shoulders sank against the soft but firm mattress. "No, I'm fine. Be sure and wake me when Aidan gets up."

Deny walked around the bed and sat down on the other side. "I will," he said as he took off his shoes then lay down next to her, close but not touching. "Sleep well, my angel," he murmured softly.

Elizabeth had thought she'd be too self-conscious and tense to fall asleep, but the last thing she remembered was the touch of his hand as it clasped hers on the bed between them.

Chapter Six

Denis woke slowly, drifting in the netherworld of semi-consciousness but aware of the soft, warm body curled backward against him in his arms. Even before he was awake enough to remember, he knew it was Elizabeth. No way could he be confused about that. Her body was almost as familiar to him as his own, and he'd spent too many lonely nights in torment, aching to hold her just like this, to be mistaken.

For a few minutes he lay quietly savoring the feel of her back and hips cuddled into the curve of his chest and belly, his thigh pressed between both of hers. His hand was cupped around one of her breasts, and to his dismay he realized that he was fully aroused.

Making a massive effort to relax, he opened his eyes and looked down at the head of tangled titian curls nestled against his chest just under his chin. She had the sexiest damn hair! He gritted his teeth to keep from rubbing his face in the soft springy mass as he'd done so often in years past. It had never failed to thrill him the way it seemed to caress his cheeks with a life of its own.

But even more exciting was the way her firm, high breast fit into his hand as if it had been made for his pleasure. She'd not only matured emotionally but physically in the three and a half years they'd been apart. She filled his palm more fully now, and he trembled with the desire to put his hand under her loose-fitting shirt and fondle the smooth warm flesh without the cotton-knit covering.

He was dammed if he was going to take advantage of her while she slept, and he sure didn't need to be aroused any more than he already was! It was all he could do to lie still and not thrust his groin against her deliciously rounded buttocks to relieve some of the throbbing need that was driving him crazy.

Again he tried to relax and think of something else. What time was it? He couldn't move his arm to look at his watch without disturbing Elizabeth, and no way was he going to do that. She'd be outraged if she woke to find him clasping her so intimately, even though he had no idea when or how it had happened.

Had he reached out to her in his sleep? Or had she come to him instinctively? Or, once their conscious inhibitions had been relaxed in slumber had they sought each other, as two halves seeking to be whole?

A glance out the window told him it was still raining and also dark, so they must have slept for at least a couple of hours. He thought of his father and wondered if Aidan was still asleep. He must be, otherwise he'd have come over and either knocked on the door or come on in. Whichever, Deny would have heard him.

His musing was disturbed when Elizabeth stretched her upper body, then shifted her hips and rubbed against him, sending a shaft of heat to his turgid loins. He only barely stifled a moan, and his fingers tightened involuntarily around her breast.

For a moment he was afraid she was waking up, but then she brushed against him again and settled more deeply into his embrace. With a little sigh, she relaxed as his arms tightened around her.

How he wanted her! In his bed, in his life, anyway he could get her. What an imbecile he'd been to think he needed to be free. Free for what? To wake up in an empty bed? To come home to an empty apartment? To date women who weren't nearly as beautiful, sweet or intelligent as the one he'd so rashly run away from?

Well, maybe "run away" was a little strong. He still felt that it wouldn't have been in their best interests to marry before they'd had time to grow up, but he should have made sure he wouldn't lose her in the process of trying to explain that. They could have continued to be best friends and sweethearts, even long-distance, until she'd finished college, but he'd blown it and now...

The jangling ring of the telephone startled him and his whole body jerked, waking Elizabeth. They rolled away from each other, and he reached for the offending instrument.

"Yeah?" he grumbled into it.

"Denis, this is Dad," said the voice on the other end of the line.

"Dad?" He blinked and swung his legs off the bed and sat up. "Why are you calling? Why don't you just come over?" For heaven's sake, he was just in the next room.

"I'm at the hospital."

"The hospital?" Deny jumped to his feet. "How'd you get to the hospital?"

Aidan laughed. "I took a cab. You were asleep when I looked in, and I sure wasn't going to disturb you."

For the first time in at least fifteen years Deny felt himself blush. Even his ears felt hot. "Yeah, well look, I hate to tell you this," he said defensively, "but that's all we were doing. Just sleeping. How is Mom doing?"

"Your mother's fine," Aidan said, and belatedly Deny recognized the jubilance in his tone. "Her temperature broke a short time ago, and she's feeling much better. She's alert and breathing more easily."

Deny felt giddy with relief. "Oh, thank God," he murmured effusively.

"Yes, thank God, indeed," echoed his father.

Elizabeth sat on the edge of the bed, battling the dizziness that came from waking and rising too fast from a sound sleep. She could hear Deny talking on the phone, but was still too dazed to make out what he was saying.

She dropped her head in her hands and took a deep breath. Good heavens, she'd really been out of it. It had been years since she'd slept so deeply. Could it have been because Deny was lying beside her?

Lifting her head, she ran her fingers through her disheveled hair. No, that didn't make sense. She'd been unwilling, anxious, about napping with him. She hadn't expected to be able to sleep at all.

Then she remembered the dream. Or rather, she *almost* remembered it. It was fleeting, illusive, but she couldn't forget the feel of loving arms around her, holding her protectively and caressing her....

The illusion faded, but not the emotions it had aroused. She'd felt so sheltered, so protected, so cherished. She'd also felt the sweet, urgent pulsing of desire, a sensation she'd never experienced with anyone but Denis O'Halloran.

Damn! She'd known it was folly to lie on the bed with him. Why had she let him talk her into it? She didn't need to be tormented by sexual stirrings she had no intention of indulging!

She heard him put the phone back in its cradle and turned to look at him. He looked as if he'd just had a huge weight lifted from him.

"Good news?" she asked uncertainly.

A happy grin transformed him. "The best. Mom's temperature is normal and she's alert and breathing easier."

His words were electrifying. She jumped up and started toward him. "Oh, Deny, that's what they've been waiting for. She should be all right now."

He met her at the foot of the bed and caught her in his arms, whirling her around in an exuberant dance. She clung to him and laughed as he pranced about the room, clutching her to him but never letting her feet touch the floor.

"Let's put our shoes back on and go over to the hospital," he said happily when he finally stopped cavorting around and put her down. "Then after we've seen Mom we'll go out for that dinner I promised you."

Elizabeth badly wanted to spend the evening with him. It was exactly what they'd have done three and a half years ago under the same circumstances, but that was the reason she couldn't do it now. They were no longer sweethearts. They weren't even friends, and that's the way she wanted to keep it. No more meals together; no more sharing a bed, no matter how chastely; no more wild, joyful clowning around like school kids.

They were no longer carefree children. Deny had seen to that when he broke her heart and left her to pick up the pieces alone. She'd lost her innocence that day, and innocence was like virginity. Once it was taken away it could never be restored. Never again would she give her heart, or her unfettered trust, to a man. Certainly not to this one!

"I'm sorry, Deny, but I have to go right home," she told him as she walked away from him and sat back down on the side of the bed. "I'll see Aunt Maggie early tomorrow morning."

"But we'd made plans to have dinner here at the hotel."

She had her back to him as she picked up one shoe, but she heard the shocked disbelief in his tone.

"No, you told your brothers not to wait dinner for you and Aidan," she said, and put on the shoe.

"I said 'don't wait dinner for *us*.' I meant the three of us, and you know it." His tone had changed from shocked to argumentative.

She picked up the other shoe and put it on. He was right, she had known he was including her. She'd even intended to go, but that was before she came to her senses again.

"I have other plans for tonight," she said firmly, and was glad her voice didn't break. "I promised Mom and Dad I'd call them again and bring them up-to-date on the fire damage. They'll be expecting it. I don't want to keep them waiting."

She finished tying her shoe and stood to find herself facing him. He looked both angry and disappointed, and before she could say anything else, he put his fingers under her chin and raised her face to look into his. "You're not going to give an inch no matter how often I apologize, are you?" he said grimly.

Why did he insist on making this so hard for her? Hadn't he hurt her enough? And why did she see pain in *his* eyes? He'd gotten what he'd wanted, his freedom.

"No, I'm not," she said slowly. "You're just making things harder for both of us. I've told you that I've forgiven you for backing out of the wedding. A loveless marriage would have been untenable after a while...."

"It wouldn't have been loveless—"

"Oh, please, stop trying to spare my feelings," she snapped, giving vent to her slow-building anger. "And stop lying to me. That's what caused all the problems in the first place. The least you can do is be truthful."

"I'm not lying, dammit!" He was as angry as she. "I've never lied to you, but for some reason you don't want to believe that. How can I tell you the truth when you won't listen?"

She twisted away from him and picked up her purse from the bar. "I have listened, Deny," she said, more gently this time. "Maybe you really believe what you're telling me, but don't you see? That just makes it worse. It's bad enough for you to lie to me, but if you're lying to yourself because you don't want to admit that you never did love me, then that's all the more reason for me to stay as far away from you as I can get."

She opened her purse and rummaged in it for her car keys. "There's an old saying that I read somewhere. *'If you fool me once, shame on you, but if you fool me twice then shame on me.'* Well, I've had all the shame thrust on me that I intend to suffer. I've no intention of letting you hurt me again, ever."

She turned and walked out of the suite and down the hall, where she caught the elevator just before the door closed.

Elizabeth waited until nine o'clock that night to call her parents in Cairo. It would be early morning there, and she knew they wouldn't leave their room until they heard from her. It was her mother who answered, but they were both listening in, sharing the phone receiver.

"Elizabeth, we've been waiting for your call. Before you say anything else, tell us how Maggie is."

Elizabeth told her what Aidan had said, and Kathleen sighed with relief. "Oh, thank the Lord. I've been so worried."

"I know you have, Mom. We all have. She should be all right now, though. The drop in temperature means the medication has finally kicked in and is doing what it's supposed to. I haven't seen her yet, but I will first thing in the morning."

"Be sure to give her our love," Kathleen said fervently, then changed the subject. "Now, tell us about the fire."

Elizabeth winced. This news wasn't going to be so happy. "All the statistics have escalated since I last talked to you," she said slowly. "Damage is estimated to be around two billion dollars, but it might not be over yet. It's raining, and the city engineers are afraid of mud slides if it keeps up. The hills have been stripped of trees and vegetation, and a heavy amount of rain will bring erosion, and mud-and-debris flows."

Kathleen moaned, and Connor's voice was muffled with despair. "Is there no end to this horror? Where are the people living who were burned out?"

Elizabeth slowly shook her head although no one was there to see. "I don't know, Dad. The Red Cross has set up temporary shelters, but they're jammed. More than three thousand houses and apartments were destroyed. Some, like the O'Hallorans, have relatives they can stay with, others are trying to rent, but a lot of unscrupulous landlords are exploiting the tragedy by rent gouging. I've heard rumors that some are charging up to a thousand dollars above what it should be."

They talked for several more minutes, and Elizabeth eventually managed to switch the conversation away from the tragedy in Oakland and over to her parents' trip from

Greece to Egypt and their impressions of Cairo and the hotel where they were staying.

"You two try not to dwell on what's going on here," she advised as she prepared to hang up. "There's nothing you can do about it, and worrying won't help. Enjoy the rest of your vacation, and don't be in any hurry to come home. I doubt that I'll be able to find a suitable place for you to live in Oakland or Berkeley, anyway. I've been thinking, with Dad retired, you really don't have to live in the Bay Area. Maybe you should think about spending the winter in Palm Springs, or even Arizona."

Although they protested that they couldn't do that, Elizabeth hoped that the seed she'd planted in their minds would germinate as time went by. After agreeing to call them again the following night, or morning in their case, she told them she loved them and broke the connection.

The following day Maggie was moved out of intensive care, and the day after that, Sunday, she was released from the hospital, just a week after being admitted.

Elizabeth hadn't seen Deny since she left the hotel Friday night, and her emotions were ambivalent. She'd been afraid he'd come to the trauma center and try to talk to her, but when he didn't, she felt abandoned.

Make up your mind, lady, she chastized herself. You damn him if he does, and damn him if he doesn't. What's the matter with you, anyway? You can't have it both ways.

She'd visited Maggie early each morning before any of the family members arrived, and phoned the nurses' station for a progress report each afternoon before leaving. When she learned on Sunday that the patient had been dismissed to be taken to her daughter's home in San Francisco, Elizabeth was overjoyed, but almost immediately her happiness was replaced with the leaden feeling of emptiness that had plagued her after Deny left her practically standing at the altar. He'd no longer be coming to the hospital, so it was unlikely that she'd see him again.

This time she had only herself to blame, only *blame* wasn't the right word. Obviously she'd made a wise choice in refusing to become involved with him again. If he could walk away from her without even saying goodbye or thank you for caring once the emergency with his mother was over, then his feelings for her were pretty superficial. Probably motivated more by the desire to cleanse himself of guilt, than to take up where they'd left off.

So why did she have this feeling that she'd made a big mistake by insisting that he leave her alone?

She called her parents again that evening to tell them that Maggie was much better and had been released from the hospital. A message that was greeted with sobs of relief from Kathleen, and a lot of throat clearing from Connor. But, unfortunately, she had to follow up with the bad news that there had been another fire-related death, bringing the total to twenty-five.

"That's terrible. Terrible," Connor muttered sadly. "Are you sure you don't need us there to handle some of the legalities? What do you hear from the insurance company?"

"Everything's proceeding as orderly as possible, Dad," Elizabeth answered. "The insurance company has appraisers working on it, but with hundreds of claims it will take months to settle them all. Meanwhile, all we can do is wait, so there's no need for you to hurry back."

They talked for a little longer, and just as she was saying goodbye, the doorbell rang. She was using the phone in her bedroom, but she heard Pilar answer the door.

As Elizabeth hung up, her apartment mate appeared in the open doorway. "There's someone here to see you," she announced with a big grin.

"Oh? Who?" Elizabeth asked, surprised because she seldom had unexpected callers, but Pilar had already disappeared and Elizabeth could hear her talking to someone in the living room.

A quick glance in the mirror assured her that she looked presentable in the fawn slacks and teal-green shirt she'd worn to work that day. She hurried across the hall to stop, stunned, when she saw Deny standing by the picture window in the living room as he talked with Pilar.

He looked at Elizabeth and smiled uncertainly. "Hello, honey. Sorry to break in on you like this, but I was afraid if I called first you wouldn't see me."

"How...how did you find out where I live?" was the only thing her confused mind could think to say as she devoured him hungrily with her gaze.

He *hadn't* just walked out of her life again without so much as a goodbye! Her relief was so great that her knees trembled.

His smile faded. "I have my ways. You didn't really think you could hide from me, did you? I don't want to be a nuisance, but I couldn't go back to Washington without trying again to put things straight between us."

The emptiness she'd been feeling turned to a sinking sensation. He was leaving again. But of course he was. There was no reason for him to stay here now that his mother was recovering. He had a job and a life in Washington that he had to get back to.

"Have you...?" She stopped and cleared her throat, then started again. "Have you met my roommate, Pilar Ignacio?" She motioned toward Pilar, who was standing beside him.

Deny looked at Pilar, too, and smiled. "Yes, we introduced ourselves when she invited me in. You didn't tell me that you shared your apartment with someone."

"Actually, Pilar shares the place with me," Elizabeth explained. "When I started working at Sisters of Mercy I needed somewhere to live, and her roommate, who was also a nurse, had left to work at a clinic for Hispanic farm workers in the rural San Joaquin Valley so Pilar invited me to move in. It's worked out beautifully, at least it has for me."

Elizabeth realized that she was chattering in an effort to fill up any awkward silence with words, and she took a deep breath to help control her nervousness.

"For me, too." Pilar spoke to Deny. "Liz is an angel to live with. She never complains about anything, and she even eats my spicy cooking."

She grinned, then turned. "Now, if you'll excuse me, I'll take the laundry downstairs and do it."

"Oh, but you don't need to—"

"Thanks, Pilar." Deny interrupted Elizabeth's protest. "Half an hour is about all I need. Forty-five minutes max."

"You got it," Pilar said, and walked toward the bathroom where they kept the laundry hamper.

After she left the apartment, Elizabeth and Deny eyed each other warily. "You may have forgotten, but I don't give up easily," he reminded her.

She sighed as she walked over to the couch and sat down. "When are you leaving?"

He raised an eyebrow. "Leaving?"

"Going back to Washington."

"Oh, that. I'm not sure. It depends on how Mom gets along now that she's out of the hospital."

He paused, and his voice became more intimate. "It also depends on how long it takes me to convince you that I'm telling the truth when I say I want you to be my sweetheart again."

"Wouldn't that be a little difficult with three thousand miles between us?" There was a touch of sarcasm in her tone.

He leaned toward her and caught her gaze with his. "I didn't come here to spar with you, Elizabeth. I came to invite you to dinner at Rosalie's tomorrow night. The whole family will be there, and we want you with us. I'll pick you up. Is six-thirty too early?"

She knew that was a bad idea, but her regrettable longing to be with him and his family was stronger than her unreliable sense of caution. Still, she had to try. "Oh, Deny, I don't—"

"Don't be stubborn, Elizabeth." His tone was gentle but firm. "If you don't want to go with me, then Dad will pick you up. He had Seamus help him select a new car to replace the ones that were burned up, and he's dying to put some miles on it."

Deny reached out and put his hand over hers where it lay on the cushion between them. "Our families are just starting to get back on a friendly basis, but it will be difficult to heal the past if you and I aren't speaking."

She didn't answer immediately. What he said was true, and she really did want to spend the evening with him and his family away from the hospital. She hadn't even seen his sister, Rosalie, and her family yet.

It was time to admit that she'd nurtured her pain and wounded pride long enough. That she would never really heal until she stopped feeling sorry for herself and put the whole unhappy episode behind her. The only way she could do that was to admit Deny back into her life as a friend.

Surely the sexual tension between them was merely a residue from their former relationship. Once he was back in Washington there wouldn't be any problem. If he wanted to spend time with her during the rest of his stay in Oakland, what harm could it do? It would only be for three or four days at the most, and then she could put him out of her thoughts, and life would be serene again. Wouldn't it?

She swallowed a few lingering misgivings and smiled at Deny. "I'd love to have dinner with you and your family tomorrow night. You can pick me up anytime after six."

The next day Elizabeth left work on time and hurried home to bathe and dress for her date with Deny. She kept telling herself that it wasn't a date, that she'd been invited by his family and he was just being a gentleman by picking her up. But her heart didn't believe her, and her excitement was palpable.

She soaked away the tension and fatigue of the busy day in a warm, leisurely, apple-blossom-scented bubble bath, then wrapped herself in a thick towel and applied her makeup. Like most redheads, she had smooth, creamy skin with a natural blush to the cheeks that made artificial color unnecessary. A touch of eye shadow, and a brushing of mascara to darken her light eyelashes, plus a shade of lipstick that complemented the highlights in her hair was all she needed.

Sometimes she added a dusting of powder in an effort to make the sprinkling of freckles across her nose less noticeable, but Deny had always objected when she did that. He said they were the visible proof that she was a mischievous redheaded leprechaun put on earth to bedevil him, so she didn't bother with it tonight. Would he remember? Probably not.

Pilar came in to help her dress, and they promptly got into an argument over what she should wear. Elizabeth selected a tailored skirt and blouse that Pilar vetoed as too businesslike. Then she found a low-cut velvet gown that Elizabeth rejected as too dressy. They finally settled on a turquoise silk jumpsuit worn with matching high-heeled sandals and several gold chains in graduating lengths at the partially unbuttoned neckline.

"That's just right," Pilar said as Elizabeth turned in a circle for her inspection. "It's a beautiful outfit, and the color really sets off your hair. How come I've never seen you wear it before?"

Elizabeth had to admit that it was just the look she'd been aiming for. "I don't know. It's too dressy to wear to work or out shopping, and I haven't been dating much."

"That's an understatement," Pilar said. "You turn down nearly all the guys who ask you out, and when you do go it's never with the same fellow twice. Does this mean that you're going to make up with Deny?"

Elizabeth hesitated. "It means we're going to be friends, but that's all. Besides, he's leaving in a few days."

When Deny arrived, he closed the door behind him and for a long moment his sober gaze roamed over her. "I think I came to the wrong house," he finally said, his voice low and husky. "You can't be the little girl I used to know who dressed like Alice in Wonderland in ruffles, and ribbons, and bows."

Elizabeth wasn't sure if he was teasing or serious. "Are you disappointed?"

Slowly he shook his head. "I'm overwhelmed. I've always known you were beautiful, but I wasn't prepared to see you looking so...so sleek and sophisticated."

He put out his hand and fingered the springy curls that Pilar had pulled back on the sides and anchored with gold-and-turquoise clips. "I've got to tell you, sweetheart, those uniforms you wear at the hospital don't do you justice."

Elizabeth saw the warmth in his eyes and knew he was at least partially teasing. "I'll relay your complaint to the administrator. He'll be crushed. Maybe he'll let me come to work in this."

For a moment his expression hardened. "Over my dead body," he grated, then he smiled and took her arm. "Come on. We'd better get out of here before I say or do something to make you run away from me again."

Rosalie's husband, Victor Quinlan, was a journalist whose popular column was syndicated in influential newspapers all over the country. For a man not yet forty, he had the knack of grappling with issues, both large and small, and presenting them to the readers in a down-to-earth way that caught their attention and made them think.

The Quinlans lived in a big white Italianate-style home in the Pacific Heights district of San Francisco, and Elizabeth had always been intrigued by the half columns, the huge urns and the long stone staircase on the outside of the building. She and Deny were greeted by Rosalie, a younger version of Maggie with dark hair and sky-blue eyes, who grabbed Elizabeth in an excited hug.

"Well, it's about time," she said happily. "I've been hearing all about you, but the two times I was able to visit Mom at the hospital you weren't around. Let me look at you." She held Elizabeth at arm's length. "God, how you've changed. They tell me you're a nurse, but you look more like a model."

She put her arm around Elizabeth's waist and started walking toward the living room. "Come on in and say hello to the rest of the gang, then I'll take you to the family room and turn all the O'Halloran grandkids loose on you. You probably won't recognize any of them they've grown so much."

Elizabeth was so completely caught up and surrounded by the big, close-knit O'Halloran family from then until dinner was announced that she only managed rare glimpses of

Deny. Maggie was dressed but ensconced in a lounge chair with portable oxygen equipment by her side in case the excitement or the lack of oxygen in the air from the milling crowd should make it hard for her breathe.

Elizabeth knelt and hugged her. "Oh, Aunt Maggie, it's so good to see you feeling well again. You look just great. Your color's back to normal, and I love that caftan you're wearing. The blue just matches your eyes."

"Ah, Elizabeth," Maggie said, "it's wonderful having you back with us again. The family gatherings just weren't the same without you."

Later, in the family room, Elizabeth was amazed at how much the assembled children had changed in three and a half years. "I don't see your two oldest kids," she said to Seamus's wife, Jill. "Didn't they come with you?"

Jill laughed. "Heather's married and Michael's in college."

"No. They can't be," Elizabeth gasped.

"Oh, but they are," Jill assured her. "The other three are still at home, though, as you just saw."

"I understand Glendon's still not married," Elizabeth said, refering to Deny's bachelor brother. "Do you suppose he'll ever make that commitment? He's not getting any younger."

Jill shrugged. "You know Glen. His life revolves around his paintings and that gallery. His women come and go, but I doubt that any of them would seriously consider playing second fiddle to his art."

Finley's wife, Lucy, wandered over with a golden-haired toddler in her arms, and leading another one just like the first by the hand.

"The nanny's rounding up the smaller kids to feed them in the playroom upstairs," she informed them. "Have you seen my other two?"

Jill pointed across the room at a boy about five and a girl slightly older. "They're over there. I'll get them. The nanny has Rosalie's two older ones, and my teenagers have graduated to eating in the dining room with the adults."

By the time they had all the children assembled and eating in the playroom, dinner was announced for the adults in the dining room. Deny scowled as he spotted Elizabeth coming down the stairs with his sisters-in-law, and took her by the arm when she drew near.

"Where have you been?" he growled quietly. "I've been looking all over for you. You took off as soon as we got here, and I haven't seen you since. I was about to send a posse out to track you down."

He sounded upset, and Elizabeth realized she'd been rude. "I'm sorry," she said contritely. "I'm afraid I sort of got absorbed in the crowd. By the time I'd finished saying hello to everybody, Jill and Lucy came to take me to the family room to see the children. I didn't realize you'd be concerned if I left you alone for a while. It never bothered you in the past."

"That was before you started walking out on me all the time." His tone was sulky, but she heard the hurt in it, too.

Without debating the advisability of her action, she reached up and stroked his cheek. "Deny, I'm sorry." Her voice was unintentionally seductive. "Truly I am, but I don't run away and hide from my problems. If I'm angry with you, I'll tell you so and then leave. I'd never sneak off and just disappear."

With a low groan he put his arms around her and held her close. "You've got me in such a state that I can't even think straight," he murmured, and nuzzled the sensitive hollow at the side of her throat, sending tiny shivers up and down her spine.

For a moment Elizabeth hesitated, fighting the irresistible urge to return his embrace. Then, giving in to the
temptation she could no longer curb, she slid her arms
around his neck and caressed the back of his head and the
bare flesh of his nape under his shirt collar. It was as if the
past three years had never happened, and she reveled in the
throbbing heat of desire that swept through her when he
lowered his hand and molded her intimately against the
hardness of his need for her.

Chapter Seven

Elizabeth didn't know how long they just stood there holding each other before a voice filled with amusement spoke from behind them, "Uncle Deny, I hate to break this up, but everyone's waiting for you two in the dining room."

Startled, they jumped apart and looked around to see Seamus and Jill's fifteen-year-old son grinning at them. "Grandpa sent me to find out what happened to you." He chuckled gleefully. "You want me to tell him?"

Elizabeth felt herself blushing, but Deny laughed and punched his young nephew good-naturedly on the arm. "Smart aleck kid," he muttered affectionately. "Just you wait, I'll get you for this, and no, I don't want you to tell your grandpa what you saw. We wouldn't want to embarrass the lady now, would we?"

"Of course not," the young man said with mock seriousness. "But you're gonna owe me."

Deny put one arm around Elizabeth's waist and the other across his nephew's shoulders and started walking toward the dining room. ''What I'm gonna owe you, buddy, is a kick in the posterior if you so much as open your mouth.''

They were all three laughing as they took their places at the table.

Aidan was given the honorary host's seat at the head, and Maggie was seated in the hostess's place at the foot. Deny and Elizabeth sat side by side, and with fourteen chairs altogether they were crowded so close that his right thigh rested against her left one.

It was distracting enough when they tried to ignore it, but as the meal progressed, Deny gave up trying and put his hand about midway between her knee and her hip under the table. His touch had all the power of a quick electrical shock, and her muscles under his palm twitched as she gave him a warning glance. He grinned and ignored it.

The silk material of her jumpsuit was lightweight and slippery, and she wore nothing but brief panties and a bra under it. His warm palm seemed to burn right through the flimsy barrier and into her quivering flesh as she fought to keep her expression neutral, but she didn't protest. She couldn't. It felt too good!

Thank heaven, he didn't caress or stroke her but just let his hand lie tantalizingly still, arousing her but also sending the message that, while he couldn't resist touching her, he wouldn't go any further until she let him know that she wanted him to.

Wanted him to! She ached with wanting. She wanted to put her hand on his leg and let her fingers wander and probe and massage, but she knew better than to start something that she couldn't, wouldn't even want to, stop.

He'd enjoyed having her tease him like that when they were engaged, but now it would only be a wanton and frustrating act that they'd both regret later.

As was usual when the multigenerational O'Halloran family got together, the meal was plentiful and delicious. When the last of the tender, succulent prime rib roast, scalloped potatoes, and various vegetables and salads had been consumed, they were served dessert and coffee in the living room. This time Deny and Elizabeth sat together on one of the couches, but still he'd managed to position them so their hips and thighs touched although, without the cover of the table and the overhanging cloth, he was forced to keep his hands to himself.

When they'd all finished their German chocolate cream pie, a luscious concoction of chocolate filling combined with coconut and chocolate chips then topped with whipped cream, Rosalie brought the baby downstairs so everyone could see him before she turned him over to the nanny to be put to bed.

Victor, the proud father, came to stand beside her, and the others all crowded around to ooh and aah and coo at the child, and comment on what a pretty baby he was and who they thought he looked like. That point was never agreed on since each had a different opinion.

Being an only child, Elizabeth had had little experience with babies, but she could never resist picking them up and holding them if the opportunity presented itself. When the crowd around Rosalie thinned Elizabeth approached her. "May I...that is, would you trust me to hold him for a few minutes?"

Rosalie chuckled. "Of course you may hold him. After all, you held my other two when they were tiny. Why don't you sit over there in the rocker and I'll hand him to you."

When Elizabeth and the child were seated in the old-fashioned pine rocking chair by the fireplace, Rosalie walked away and left them alone. Elizabeth couldn't remember what they'd named the baby, but as she looked down at the squirming bundle in her arms, her heart melted.

He was a little doll. Only eight days old, but he weighed nine pounds, was twenty-one inches long, and had chubby arms and legs and a shadow of a smile.

She put her slender finger against his hand, and he closed his tiny fist around it and hung on. She felt the tug all the way to her heart. Such a precious gift from God. How blessed Rosalie and Victor were to have three perfect children.

The filmy little eyelids closed, and Elizabeth settled more comfortably against the back of the chair and began to rock. An ethereal sense of peace stole over her, blocking out everything but the immense pleasure of cradling this new little being in her arms. He seemed to fit so naturally against her breast, and she had an overwhelming desire to be able to nourish him.

An unexpected sob rose in her throat, and she swallowed it back. This could have been her child. Hers and Deny's if they'd been married as planned. They'd both wanted a big family. Deny because he'd been raised in the bosom of one, and she, because she'd never had brothers and sisters.

Yes, surely they'd have had one baby by now, possibly even two, but would that have been wise? They'd both been young and spoiled and used to having their own way. Could they have been good parents when they were still so immature themselves?

If they'd married and had children it's unlikely she'd have continued her schooling and received her degree in nursing. The possibility of her ever having to support herself and her children alone was slim, but her R.N. gave her an independence she could never have achieved if she'd depended on either Deny or her parents for her livelihood.

It was her immaturity and dependency that had driven Deny away, but no man would ever again walk out on her for that reason. Now she didn't need anybody. She could take care of herself and any children she might have, except there might never be babies for her— Deny's or any other man's—and that was a void that no career, no matter how satisfying, could ever fill.

Her dream of a husband and family of her own had died that one dreadful summer, snuffed out by the mortification of being deserted right before her wedding by the man that everyone knew she'd been in love with all her life. It had been devastating, and she'd vowed never again to be put in such a debasing position.

She felt a tear fall from the corner of her eye, and she blinked in an effort to hold back the others that misted her vision. As she moved her head, she saw Deny sitting a few feet away in a chair, watching her. There was a look of unutterable sadness on his face.

Was he remembering and having regrets, too?

Deny was indeed having regrets. The same ones he'd been having for years, only now another one had been resurrected to torment him.

That should have been his son in Elizabeth's arms.

He wanted sons and daughters and grandchildren, but not with just any woman. Elizabeth, with her sweet smile and gentle touch, was meant to be the mother of his children. Only how could he convince her of that after the way he'd treated her in the past? She only barely tolerated him.

Still, he did seem to be making some headway. She'd let down her guard enough to nap with him the other day, and she'd come here with him tonight. If only they could be alone together some place where he could take her in his arms and tell her how miserable he's been all these years, how stupid he was to ever have doubted his need for her, and how desperately he wanted her for his wife.

But she saw to it that they were almost never alone. They only got together in crowded hospital waiting rooms or public restaurants or family gatherings such as this one where there was no chance to talk privately.

Even so, he'd tried to tell her how he felt, but she always refused to listen or to believe him.

The only glimmer of hope he had was her admission that there had been no other men for her since they had been apart. He'd tried to tell her that there had been no other women for him, either, but she hadn't wanted to hear it.

He brought his attention back to the madonna tableau just a few feet from him. Elizabeth watched the baby in her arms with a combination of tenderness and wonder usually reserved for new mothers. She stroked the soft downy hair on the little head, and her eminently kissible lips formed words he couldn't hear but must have been pleasing to the child because he flailed his tiny arms at her.

A wave of longing so strong and painful that he had to clench his jaws to keep from crying out washed over him, and he knew he could never let her get away from him again. He had to keep trying to make her understand how much he loved her, but there was a huge stumbling block in his way.

It would take time and patience to convince her to trust him enough to listen to him, and time was the one thing he didn't have. He was in the middle of a vitally important project at work and he needed to return to Washington at the earliest possible moment.

It was then that he saw Elizabeth raise her free hand to rub at her eyes and realized that she was wiping away tears. That did it! He'd had all he could take. If they were both miserable, then there had to be some way they could resolve their differences and acknowledge their love, and he was damn well going to find it.

Even though Elizabeth's attention was focused on the baby, she was vividly aware of Deny's penetrating gaze, and her heart sped up when he rose and walked over to crouch down in front of her. He put his hands on the arms of the rocker to stop its movement and looked at her with an openly tender expression.

"We can still make beautiful babies together," he said softly, as though he'd been reading her mind.

"I'm sure we could have," she answered stiffly.

"I didn't say 'could have,' sweetheart, I said 'can.' We don't have to scrap all our plans just because I was a jerk three years ago. Won't you give me another chance?"

Elizabeth's eyes widened with astonishment. Was he once again proposing marriage? Surely not. He couldn't be so insensitive as to think she'd give him another crack at destroying her.

"I don't know what you have in mind, Deny, but I'm going to pretend you didn't say that," she said grimly.

She saw him wince and his expression quickly changed to a mask of indifference. "Sorry," he said hoarsely as he stood and walked away.

Rosalie came to retrieve her little son a few minutes later. For the rest of the evening, Elizabeth and Deny put on a good show of being friendly and happy, but the wall of disappointment and distrust that for a brief time had been set aside now loomed bleakly between them again.

Even on the way home they kept up the charade with light conversation about the family: how good everyone looked, how the children had grown, and how wonderful it was to have Maggie out of the hospital and looking so well. Anything to keep from acknowledging the tension that hovered cloyingly around them, making them self-conscious and miserable.

Back in Oakland, Deny parked at the curb a short distance from Elizabeth's apartment and walked with her to the door of the big old Victorian building that had been remodeled into two small apartments on the first floor and one larger one on the second. Pilar and Elizabeth lived upstairs.

Deny unlocked the front door and gave her back her keys, but when she turned to say good-night, he spoke first. "May I come in for a few minutes? We do need to talk, something we can't do in a room full of people."

Her first impulse was to say no, but that would only prolong the agony. If there were some way they could resolve this latest tension between them, she was willing to give it a try.

"All right," she said, and led the way up the old-fashioned staircase to their left.

The apartment had originally been rented furnished, but little by little Pilar had replaced the worn items with reproductions of the Victorian period to blend with the architecture of the house. Since Elizabeth had moved in, she'd added several antique pieces that belonged to her family, and, since the fire, were now the only heirlooms remaining. The total effect was charming and homey, especially in the shadowy glow of the tiffany lamp left burning on the table in front of the lace-curtained front bay window.

"Won't you sit down?" she said as she slid the black metallic sheer woolen stole from her shoulders and upper arms. "I'll check to see if Pilar's home then be right back."

A few minutes later, she returned to find Deny sitting in one of two lounge chairs on either side of the lamp table.

"Pilar's asleep so I shut her door," Elizabeth explained. "Would you like some coffee?"

She hadn't meant to sound so stiff and formal, but that's the way it came out.

Deny shook his head. "No. All I want is for you to sit down, relax, and talk to me."

She sat down in the twin chair, but relaxing was impossible. What did he want to talk about? Was it something that would set off another argument? She hated quarreling with him, but it seemed to be the only way they could communicate anymore.

"Elizabeth, I'm sorry if I offended you earlier." His tone was soft but firm. "That wasn't my intention. I just..."

He left the rest of the sentence hanging and waved his hand as if to blow the thought away, like drifting smoke.

"Never mind," he said absently, then changed the subject. "When is your next day off from work?"

"My next day off?" she parroted. He'd surprised her. She hadn't expected that question. "Why it's..." She had to stop and think. "It's day after tomorrow, Wednesday, but we're so busy that I may have to work...."

"Don't do it," he grated. "You're entitled to two days a week off, and you need to get away from that hospital and have some fun." His tone gentled as he went on. "Let's both take a mini-vacation and go to the Napa Valley. We'll leave here early and catch the champagne flight in one of the hot-air balloons, then drive around and visit some of the wineries, and in the evening take the dinner excursion on the Wine Train. How does that sound to you?"

It sounded like heaven. The Napa Valley, north of Oakland, was the heart of the wine country in California. It was also well-known as a headquarters for picturesque giant balloon rides, wine-tasting excursions, and a restaurant train that served lunch and dinner in restored Pullman dining cars while it wound up and down the valley.

Maybe Deny was right. If they spent a whole day alone together just having fun, they might be able to smooth out their stormy relationship and be more comfortable with each other. Besides, she hadn't been to the Napa Valley in years, and he was sure right about one thing: they both needed a respite from all the stress and strain they'd been under.

"It sounds like fun," she said with a big smile. "Let's do it. We'll have to get a really early start, though, if we're going to take a balloon ride. They lift off shortly after daybreak."

On Wednesday morning Elizabeth rose at four o'clock and was dressed in jeans and a white sweatshirt with a bouquet of bright red tulips painted across the front by the time Deny arrived at four-fifteen.

"You look wide-awake and ready for a long day," he greeted her as she opened the front door for him.

"I am," she said emphatically, making no effort to stifle a big grin. "I haven't been up in a balloon since the last time I went with you when I was a freshman in college."

"Neither have I," he replied as they climbed the stairs to her apartment. "It's a beautiful day for it. No fog and no wind, and I doubt that it will be any different in Napa."

"Pilar's still asleep," Elizabeth said as they entered the living room, "but I have my change of clothes for this evening right here so I won't have to disturb her."

She motioned to a garmet bag lying across the back of a chair, and Deny picked it up and slung it over his shoulder. "My things are in the car. If you're ready we'd better be on our way. We're to meet the rest of the passengers at Marie Callender's restaurant on the other side of Napa at five-thirty."

It was still dark, and the sky was aglow with stars as they began their forty-something-mile trip up Interstate 80.

Traffic at this hour of the morning was no problem, and Deny's rented sportscar was fast and smooth, like floating through the night. The music of Rick Springfield surrounded them in stereo, and Elizabeth recognized it as a tape that had been a special favorite of hers before she and Deny broke up.

"Where . . . where did you get that tape," she asked, and hoped he hadn't noticed the catch in her voice.

He glanced at her, then reached over and took her hand. "I couldn't find it for sale in any of the shops so I borrowed this one from Rosalie. I remember how much you used to enjoy it."

She squeezed his hand. "That was . . ." She paused and swallowed back the lump in her throat. "That was very thoughtful of you. I haven't heard it in a long time."

She hadn't listened to her copy since Deny left because he'd given it to her and she knew it would only make her cry. But now, listening to it with him again, she felt a sweet nostalgia rather than sadness.

At Vallejo Deny turned off onto Highway 29 and headed toward the wine country. Elizabeth's excitement mounted. "Was there any problem getting reservations so late?" she asked.

"Not really. I had to try a couple of balloon companies before I found one with space, and the Wine Train is always booked up well in advance for lunch, but they were able to fit us in for the dinner excursion. I also reserved us a room at a motel that Finley recommended."

Elizabeth froze. *"A motel room?"*

Her tone was icy, and he turned a startled look at her. "Now hold on, honey," he said anxiously. "There are a lot of other things to do in a motel room besides make love. This is going to be a long day, and we'll need a place to rest, freshen up and change clothes before dinner. I even ordered two double beds so you could have one all to yourself if you want to take a nap. Dammit, Elizabeth, I have every intention of driving you back to Oakland tonight if that's what's bothering you."

She relaxed and felt like a fool. Why was she always jumping to conclusions with Deny? All her life, until the aborted wedding, she'd trusted him without question. She'd have laid her life on the line if he'd asked her to, but now she couldn't even seem to give him the benefit of the doubt.

She slumped back against the seat and closed her eyes. "I'm sorry," she said on an involuntary shudder. "You're right, of course. I just wasn't thinking straight."

She could feel the tension that radiated from him as he clutched the steering wheel and looked straight ahead. "No, you weren't," he answered tightly. "Elizabeth, have I ever, at any time, forced or seduced you into doing something you didn't want to do?"

She heard both hurt and anger in his tone, and she reached out to put her hand on his arm. "No, never, and I know you never would."

He didn't move. "Then why won't you trust me?"

Why wouldn't she, indeed? She remembered a saying that had been a favorite of her mother's. *Don't throw out the baby with the bathwater.* Is that what she was doing? Was she throwing away a very special relationship just because she couldn't trust him to love her and take care of her?

That would be a mistake. She no longer needed a man to take care of her, she could do that herself. Marriage had no part in her plans for the future, but the lifelong friendship she and Deny had shared was too precious to be sacrificed to her pride and her silly fears.

The muscles in his arm were tense under her palm, and she leaned over and rubbed her forehead against his shoulder. It was time for her to be truthful with herself, as well as with him.

"Deny, I'm beginning to realize that it's not your motives I don't trust, it's my own reactions." Her tone was soft and her voice quivered, betraying her turbulent feelings.

He finally looked at her. "I don't understand."

She lifted her head and returned his look. "I hardly understand it myself. All I know is that it nearly killed me when you canceled the wedding and walked out of my life."

He drew a quick intake of breath. "I didn't—"

"Please, let me finish," she interrupted. "I thought I hated you, and even though over the years I came to realize that you were right, that we had been too young for marriage, I still couldn't really forgive you. Then, when I saw you again..."

She paused, trying to get her thoughts in order. "I...I don't know how to say this. From the moment you took me in your arms and we cried on each other's shoulders when we saw the devastation of the fire storm, I've been terrified."

His eyes widened with shock. "Terrified? Of me? My God, Elizabeth, you know I'd never hurt you."

She shook her head. "Not physically, no, but emotionally...well, you nearly destroyed me emotionally once, and I'll do anything to keep from being hurt that badly again."

Deny gasped. "I wouldn't—"

"Maybe not, but I'm not willing to gamble on it. That's what terrifies me. I've discovered that I don't hate you. I don't love you, either, but I do have strong feelings of tenderness and...and desire...that I'm afraid could get out of control. That's why I'm so quick to attack you when you make advances toward me.

"I don't want to take up where we left off, Deny, but neither do I want to lose your friendship. It's very dear to me.

Will you forgive me for my thorny impulses if I promise to make every effort to curb them in the future?''

To her surprise, he pulled over to the side of the nearly deserted road and shut off the motor. Although it would be some time before daylight, the blackness of night had faded enough that she could see his sober expression as he turned toward her and reached out to touch her face.

"I'd rather you didn't have any thorny impulses to curb," he said as he ran the back of his fingers down her cheek, "but you've got to know that I'll forgive you anything. Haven't I always?"

He grinned. "Remember the time you told Melanie, that blond cheerleader I was dating in high school, that I was secretly in love with a girl from another school whom my parents disapproved of, and I was only going out with Melanie so they wouldn't suspect that I was still seeing my 'true love'?" He laughed. "She dropped me like a hot potato."

Elizabeth laughed, too. "I was only fourteen and consumed with jealousy. Besides, I believed most of what I said. I fantasized that you were in love with me, but since my parents insisted I was too young to date, you were just going out with 'older women' until I became available."

Deny was once more serious as he brushed his thumb back and forth across her lips. "You were right, you know, but at the time I wasn't mature enough to understand my motivations. I was pretty teed off with you for a while, but it didn't last long and I forgave you."

The gentle friction of his thumb on her mouth made her shiver, and her lips parted as she closed her eyes. She heard his low groan just before his hands slid up to the sides of her head, and his mouth replaced his thumb on her lips.

It was like honey dripped onto parched skin. Like the overwhelming relief of water after a long, tormenting thirst. Like the taste of ambrosia at the end of a period of fasting.

Her body went limp, and she raised her arms to clasp his shoulders as she mentally cursed the bucket seats that made a full embrace impossible. It had been so long since she'd felt the gentle roughness of his mouth, the tip of his tongue caressing her lips, the fresh sweetness of his breath mingling with hers.

For a long while they clung together, touching only from the shoulders up, and when at last they pulled apart, they were both shaking. Deny's gaze held Elizabeth's, and his eyes were dark with controlled passion.

"Friends?" he whispered unsteadily.

"Friends," she agreed in a voice that quivered, but they both knew that with that one heartrending kiss their relationship had shot way past friendship.

They arrived at Marie Callender's in the small city of Napa about fifteen minutes later and were greeted by the hostess for the balloon company, then ushered to a private room where coffee and muffins were being served. After being introduced to the other assembled passengers, they were given release forms to sign while drinking their coffee and waiting for latecomers.

By six o'clock it was daylight, and the passengers were divided into two sections of eight each, the early and late flights. Deny and Elizabeth were in the early one. They followed the other six into a nearby van and were driven to a large vineyard near Yountville, a small town several miles north on Highway 29.

The colorful giant red-yellow-and-blue hot-air balloon was all ready inflated, and its pilot plus a few ground helpers were waiting for them. He introduced himself as Harry, and once all eight passengers had been boosted into the deep, handcrafted wicker gondola, the journey began.

The roar of the propane burners overhead broke the peaceful silence of the valley around them and startled Elizabeth. She jumped and clutched the polished rim of the gondola. Deny laughed and put his arm around her waist, pulling her back against him. "It's okay, honey. Those burners are noisy, but you don't have to worry about coming in contact with them. They're way above our heads."

She felt safe with his arms around her and relaxed to enjoy the ride. The takeoff was so gentle that she didn't realize they'd left the ground until she looked down and saw the helpers below waving at them. She waved back and smiled for the photographer who was snapping pictures.

There was no wind, and as they slowly ascended, the burners roared intermittently, but in between the silence was almost eerie. Even their voices didn't seem to penetrate it. Elizabeth enjoyed the sensation of floating, and listened with interest as Deny talked to the pilot.

"What kind of license is required to pilot a balloon?" he asked Harry.

"Oh, I'm F.A.A. certified for ballooning, crop dusting, aerial towing, and glider and powered flight," Harry answered.

Elizabeth felt even more relaxed after hearing that.

The view of the green mountain ranges to the east and the west and the flat valley floor covered with vineyards was magnificent. The vineyards looked like miniature rectangular gardens atop a giant table, and when they reached fifteen hundred feet they could see all the way to the San Francisco Bay as they drifted back toward Napa.

An hour later the descent was as smooth as the ascent had been, and the bottom of the gondola actually skimmed lightly over the top of the leafy grapevines just before landing in a small field on the outskirts of Napa. The other half of the original group were there and were immediately loaded into the balloon for the trip back to Yountville.

Later, at the restaurant, they were served a champagne breakfast with entrées they could order from a special menu. Elizabeth chose the quiche Lorraine, which turned out to be a whole individual pie, delicious but more than she could eat. Deny polished off the rest for her after he finished his Belgium waffle topped with strawberries and whipped cream.

They spent the rest of the morning exploring Napa's renovated "old town" section with its brick walkways, courtyards, boutiques and restored Opera House. In the early afternoon they visited some of the chateaulike wineries built of local stone before the turn of the century, where they joined guided tours of the operation and tasted the various wines.

During the day, the wind had come up, and at three o'clock Deny and Elizabeth checked into the motel, tired, windblown and a little woozy from their wine tasting. Elizabeth's quick look around assured her that the room was attractive and comfortable with all the usual furnishings, including two full-size beds and a round table with two padded chairs.

She sighed and dropped her purse onto the dresser as she walked by on her way to the bed nearest the picture window. She wasn't sure when it had happened, but at some time during the past ten hours together she'd relaxed her guard and lost the tense uneasiness that had plagued her when Deny was around. They'd been having so much fun that they'd slipped back into the old carefree bond of saying what they thought, touching when they wanted to, and engaging in the uninhibited give and take of lifelong friends. It was wonderful!

Sinking down onto the bed, she stretched and squirmed to work the kinks out of her tired muscles. "Mmm, it feels so good to lie down and relax," she murmured blissfully, and looked up at Deny, who was standing next to her. "I'm so glad you thought to reserve us a room. I should have known you'd do the right thing. You always do."

"Not always," he said sadly, and sat down on the bed beside her. He picked up her legs and put her feet in his lap, then began unfastening her sneakers.

"Are you going to massage my feet again?" she asked hopefully.

He nodded as he pulled off one shoe and sock and started on the other. "Yes."

She closed her eyes. "It will put me to sleep."

The other shoe and sock hit the floor, and he leaned down and kissed her bare instep, sending arrows of delight up her leg. "I know." He kissed her foot again then started to caress it with his strong fingers. "I want you to take a nap so you won't be too tired to enjoy dinner and the train ride."

He picked up her other foot and kissed it, too, then started rubbing it, sending matching arrows up that leg. Although it was arousing, it was also soothing, and she moaned with contentment. "Are you going to nap, too?" It was an effort to speak.

He was working on both feet at the same time now. "I might."

"Would you like to sleep on this bed with me?" She hadn't realized she was going to say that until she did, and then it was too late for regrets.

He drew in a deep breath, and his hands stilled. For a moment she was afraid she'd offended him, but then his fingers slowly repeated their magic. "Yes." He said it so softly that it was almost a whisper.

She slid her feet out of his lap and rolled over onto her side to make room for him.

Within seconds he joined her and curled himself around her back with his arm across her waist. The last thing she remembered was the touch of his lips on her neck, and his voice murmuring, "Sleep tight, my love."

Chapter Eight

Elizabeth woke to the sound of water spraying from the shower. She blinked and rolled over to discover that she was alone on the bed. A sharp twinge of disappointment annoyed her. She should be grateful that Deny'd had the good sense to get up while she still slept.

Her ambivalence on that point unsettled her. What kind of relationship did she really want with him—friendship or lovers? She was going to have to make up her mind, fast, or he'd think she was just being a tease. He wouldn't put up with this chaste sleeping together for much longer. No man would.

For that matter neither could she. She was well aware of her weakness for Deny. Next time they lay on the bed together, if he didn't make a pass she'd seduce him. She wouldn't be able to help herself. Then what?

She raised her arm and looked at her watch. Four-thirty. They were supposed to be at the train depot at six, so she'd better shower as soon as he finished. But instead of getting up she lay there listening to the splashing water. She imagined his naked male body, still tanned from the summer sun, standing under the stinging spray, black hair plastered to his head, eyes and mouth open as he reveled in the full force of it.

The picture in her mind was so clear that she failed to notice the silence when the shower was turned off, until a few minutes later when the door opened and he emerged wearing nothing but a white towel around his hips. He saw her startled expression and grinned wickedly. "Sorry. I didn't know you were awake."

He looked neither sorry nor surprised as he crossed the room to stand by the bed. "Time to rise and shine, Sleeping Beauty," he announced. "We've got a train to catch."

His teasing gaze roamed over her. "That is, unless you'd rather I came back to bed."

For a fleeting moment the urge to hold up her arms and invite him to do just that was almost irresistible, but when he fingered the knot in the towel as if to untie it, Elizabeth came to her senses and scrambled to her feet. "No! I—"

In her panic she barreled straight into him, and his arms closed tightly around her. "Now you're getting the idea," he murmured and kissed her, hard and wet and quick, then pulled away and slapped her playfully on the bottom. "Get in that bathroom and lock the door, and don't come out again until we're both fully dressed, or I won't be responsible for what happens."

He gave her a gentle shove in the right direction, and in spite of her quaking knees she managed to make it the rest of the way by herself.

They dressed, checked out of the motel and still got to the train station with time to spare. "Have you ever ridden the Wine Train before?" Deny asked as he and Elizabeth studied the framed paintings by local artists that lined the walls of the interior of the station.

"No, but I've always wanted to. Have you?"

He shook his head. "No. The few times I've come back to California since I left, there were always too many other things to do and people to visit. I spent most of my time scanning faces in the crowds hoping to catch a glimpse of you."

Elizabeth's stomach muscles clenched. "I seldom came home during those last two years of college. I lived on campus and spent most of my time at the hospital or studying. The first Christmas Dad took Mom and me to Paris, and we spent the following one in Italy."

Deny looked puzzled. "But you were home every holiday and nearly every weekend during your first two years at San Jose State. In fact, as I remember only too well, it was because you couldn't bear to leave your parents, your home, and all your friends that you wouldn't come to Washington with me. What happened?"

She grimaced. "I grew up, very suddenly and very painfully, after you dumped me—"

"Elizabeth, I did not dump you!" Denny said through gritted teeth.

Oh damn, she'd done it again! She reached for his hand. "I'm sorry. Truly I am. I didn't mean to sound so bitchy."

He squeezed her fingers. "No, don't apologize. I just wish you could understand...." He turned and clutched her by the arms. "Was it because you were afraid of running into me that you stayed away?"

She decided she might as well tell him everything. "Yes, that was part of it. Also with our parents not speaking or acknowledging each other, the atmosphere was so tense and awful." She shivered. "But mostly, I just couldn't face all those hundreds of people whom I'd had to notify when the wedding was called off.''

Deny swore and took her in his arms, apparently oblivious to all the people milling around. ''Sweetheart, I knew I'd put you in a difficult position. God knows, Dad and Mom reminded me of it every time they talked to me or wrote, but I had no idea you were going through—''

A loud voice on the PA system blared across the room. ''Please come to the front doors and get in line for boarding. Have your tickets ready.''

The message was repeated and everyone started to move. Deny hugged Elizabeth then released her and took her arm so they wouldn't become separated.

Elizabeth had read about the Napa Valley Wine Train at the time it was put into service several years ago, but even so she wasn't prepared for the elegance of the restored 1917 Pullman dining car replete with etched glass, polished brass, fine fabrics and rich mahogany.

After boarding the dining car, they were led down the richly carpeted aisle to a white linen-covered table decorated with fresh flowers and set with bone china, silver and crystal. She was glad she'd chosen to wear her mauve silk dress and amethyst necklace, and Deny looked smashing in navy slacks and a matching blazer.

The gourmet meal was delicious, the service exceptional, and the sound and movement of the train exciting. Her only regret was that the trip was made mostly in the dark so the only scenery visible from the wide windows was the lights of the small towns as they traveled lazily up the valley. But even that was a visual delight. Especially the occasional lighted estate or winery that dotted the vineyards between towns.

The dinner started with a bottle of chardonnay and exotic appetizers, then progressed through salad and entrée. Elizabeth ordered salmon stuffed with crab, and Deny chose steak cooked in a wine sauce, both served with wild rice and slightly undercooked vegetables just the way Elizabeth liked them.

When everyone had finished eating, they were invited to move into a lounge car for dessert and coffee. It proved to be as elegant as the dining car, with thickly upholstered chairs on each side that were faced toward the windows for easy viewing. The windowsills were narrow shelves just wide enough to hold dessert plates and coffee cups.

Deny sighed as he settled into the comfortable chair and patted his stomach. "That steak didn't look all that big, but it was sure filling. Must have been the rich sauce."

"If you think your steak was filling, you should have had my salmon and crab," Elizabeth said ruefully. "Even though I only managed to finish about half of it, I enjoyed every bite."

He put his hand over hers where it lay on the arm of the chair. "Are you having a good time?"

She turned her hand over so she could clasp his, too. "I'm having a wonderful time," she said dreamily. "It's been a magical day. I'm so glad you suggested it."

His glance held hers. "So am I. I was so afraid you'd refuse that I almost didn't—"

He was interrupted by the waiter holding a silver coffeepot. "Excuse me, sir. Would you and the lady like coffee or tea?"

Elizabeth self-consciously disengaged her hand from his, and they both asked for coffee. Another waiter followed with a large tray. "We have two choices of dessert," he announced. "Apple tart or chocolate mousse cake."

She wasn't sure she'd be able to eat either one but asked for the tart. Deny took the cake, and the waiter moved on.

After a couple of bites Elizabeth put down her plate, hoping to finish it later, and picked up the cup. "Deny, tell me about your life in Washington. Is the job as satisfactory as you thought it would be? Do you still spend a lot of time out of the country?'' *Do you make love to lots of beautiful and exciting women?*

The last question was the most important, but she had the good sense not to voice it.

He smiled and polished off the rest of his cake before answering. ''The job is everything I hoped it would be, but, as I tried to tell you before, if I had it to do over I'd accept the position in San Francisco and marry you.''

She couldn't deny that she liked hearing that, but she wondered if he really meant it. It was the polite thing to say, but she didn't want empty assurances. Better move on to another topic. ''Do you still travel all over the world?''

''No, I've been permanently based in Washington for over a year now, but it never was as glamorous as you make it sound. I spent most of my first two years in the oil-rich countries, Saudi Arabia and the other Persian Gulf nations. The work was interesting, but the heat, and the sand, and the poverty, to say nothing of the strange and unfamiliar cultures and traditions, were uncomfortable and depressing. I was more than ready to settle down back in the good old U.S.A.''

While they were talking, the train slowed as it reached the outskirts of St. Helena, the home of some of California's most famous wines, Beringer, Charles Krug and Christian Brothers among others. It was also the end of the line.

''Will they turn the train around?'' Elizabeth asked.

''I doubt it,'' Deny answered. ''They'll probably just hook up an engine to the other end, if they don't have one already, and reverse directions.''

That's exactly what happened, and in a short time they were headed back toward Napa.

By then they'd finished their dessert and coffee and refused the offer of more wine. "I've had as much wine today as I usually drink in a year," Elizabeth mused.

Again Deny reached out and twined her hand in his. "You didn't drink at all the last time I saw you, you weren't old enough."

"I seldom drink now, either. Only on special occasions, and today has been a *very* special one."

He lifted their clasped hands to his mouth and caressed the back of hers with his lips. "Any time spent with you is *very* special for me."

The light in the car was dim, and she didn't object when he stroked her wrist with the tip of his tongue, sending tingles up her arm. Or when he turned her hand over and planted tiny kisses in the hollow of her palm. An innocent-looking gesture that made her shiver all the way to her core.

"Deny." Her voice was a husky whisper, and she wasn't sure whether it was a whimper to stop or a plea to continue.

Fortunately, he apparently had a little more control than she did, and he brought their hands back down to one of the narrow chair arms between them before he leaned over and brushed her lips with his, setting up a magnetism that was almost impossible to break.

"I know, sweetheart," he whispered into her ear. "I'm on fire. I hope you are, too."

She nodded and heard his low groan as he took her earlobe between his lips and sucked for a moment before he released it and straightened up. "I...I think we'd better change the subject," he said shakily.

She drew in a deep breath and cast around in her muddled mind for something neutral to talk about. She wasn't sure there was such a thing when she was with Deny. No matter what they said it had heated sexual undertones.

"Uh...you...you haven't told me where you live," she finally stammered. "Do you have a condo or a house?"

"A small apartment, actually. When I was moving around so much I just needed a permanent address and a place to store my things. Since I quit traveling I find that the apartment suits my needs just fine. It's secured, the rent includes housekeeping service, and it's close to where I work."

"It sounds lonely," she murmured, then wished she could bite back the words.

He squeezed her hand. "Living alone is lonely, sweetheart." His voice was low and husky. "You're lucky to have Pilar for a roommate."

They talked little after that, just sat there holding hands and watching the shimmering stars, the darkly silhouetted hills in the distance, and the changing lights as the train rumbled slowly on through the night.

Elizabeth felt a sense of all-encompassing peace, and knew that it wasn't the gourmet dinner, or the world-class wine, or even the mesmerizing clack-clack of the train wheels that induced it. It was the gentle touch of Deny's hand enfolding hers that had the power to put her mind at rest, to make her heart swell with love and her face glow with contentment.

Deny, who had once broken her heart, was apparently the only man who could also heal it.

But could she trust him to cherish it? Or would he callously break it again at some later date?

The train arrived back in Napa at nine-thirty as scheduled, and within twenty minutes they were on the highway and headed south toward Oakland. Elizabeth settled against the soft leather upholstery of the sports car, but now that they were alone, the peacefulness she'd felt earlier had been replaced by a hot, edgy, pulsating desire that tormented her.

Apparently Deny was having the same problem, because he reached over and put his hand on her thigh. Her muscles twitched, and she squirmed with the need his touch built in her, but she didn't object.

Her skirt was short and snug and, when she was sitting, left most of her thigh uncovered. His hand rested between her knee and the hem of her dress with nothing but the cobweblike nylon of her stocking between his flesh and hers. His palm was hard and rough enough to gently snag the delicate nylon as it moved in a slow, gentle caress.

She sucked in her breath and clamped her hand over his to still it as she made a massive effort not to wriggle again. The light from the dash gave off enough illumination that she could see the satisfied half smile he turned on her, and this time she did protest. "Deny, you promised you wouldn't seduce me."

It sounded more like a plea than a rebuff.

"Am I seducing you?" His voice was low and husky.

"You know you are." Again it sounded more like an admission than a rebuke. She tried once more. "You said you wouldn't do anything I didn't want you to."

This time it was his fingers that explored, so lightly that it was more like a tickle than a caress. A tickle that reached her most intimate erogenous zone and burst into flame.

"Are you saying you don't like what I'm doing to you?" His tone didn't change, but his smile was gone.

"Yes. No. Oh damn, I don't know." How could she think when she was drowning in erotic sensations?

"I'll stop if you want me to," he said raggedly, "but sitting so close to you in the dark is a powerful temptation. Not being able to touch you would be just plain hell."

How could she resist him when he talked like that? "For me, too," she admitted, "but what happens when we get back to Oakland?"

His restless hand moved again, rubbing back and forth on her leg. "We've been in this situation before, sweetheart. Do I have to remind you what happened later?"

A wave of heat made her moan as her sensitized memory came flooding back. "No!" It was a cry of frustration rather than a straight answer. "That's not the same. We were engaged then."

She knew she wasn't making sense. How could she when her brain was melting along with the rest of her body?

In a seemingly involuntary gesture his fingers dug into her flesh. "Nothing has changed for me, Elizabeth. You're still my girl, my love. You always have been."

How could she argue with him when she wanted so badly what he was offering?

She loved him. She'd told herself that he'd killed that love when he walked out on her, but she knew now that wasn't true. She'd been hurt, humiliated, confused, and the blind trust she'd had in him was shattered beyond repair, but she'd never stopped loving him. He was so much a part of her that she couldn't be really whole without him, so why fight it?

She must have hesitated too long, because he spoke and startled her. "Honey, are you all right?"

No, she wasn't all right. If she were she'd tell him good-bye tonight and make it stick. She'd find a nice, trustworthy man and marry him. But she wasn't going to do that. Instead she was going to stifle the puritan conscience that was screaming warnings at her and deliberately choose a way of life that was foreign to everything she'd been taught about home and family and moral values.

"Elizabeth?" Deny sounded anxious. "Have I made you mad at me again? Look, if you don't want—"

He lifted his hand from her thigh, finally breaking through her trance.

"No, please," she exclaimed, and caught it in midair, then put it back where it had been. "I like for you to stroke me." She hesitated, then asked, "May I do the same for you?"

He blinked and stared at her as if trying to understand what she'd said. "P . . . please do," he stammered, then seemed to get his bearings. "Oh, sweetheart, please do."

Shyly she reached over and put her hand on his leg. The contact sent tremors through her. The wool of his slacks was finely woven, firm but not rough, and the muscles beneath it were tense and hard. They had developed with age, too, as well as the ones in his upper body. He'd always been distinctly masculine even as a boy, but there was nothing boyish about him now.

Gently she rubbed her palm back and forth, as he had done to her, and was rewarded with the feel of muscles clenching and unclenching under her hand. A happy smile tilted the corners of her mouth. He was responding to her as strongly as he always had.

Deny swallowed back a cry of exuberance when Elizabeth's small hand made contact with the top of his thigh. It felt so good, but the reflexes it aroused in him were almost unbearably urgent. He was going to need all the control he could muster.

He'd waited so long for the remembered thrill of her touch, and he'd been terrified that he'd never experience it again.

When she started caressing him, his belly tightened and he clutched the steering wheel with his free hand, grateful that there wasn't much traffic on the road at this time of night.

They traveled in silence, letting their hands convey titillating messages they were too apprehensive to voice. Deny wanted to tell her how much he loved her, to beg her to give him another chance and marry him, be his wife, the mother of his children, but that was a mine field he couldn't explore until he had some assurance that, at the very least, she wouldn't turn on him and banish him from her life forever.

When at last they veered off the freeway in Oakland, Deny's already tight stomach muscles knotted with uncertainty. In a few minutes he was going to have to make an almost impossible decision. The route to his hotel was directly ahead, but to get to her apartment, he would have to turn right.

They hadn't actually settled the question of what they were going to do when they got back there. If he assumed she wanted to spend the night at the hotel with him and he was wrong, she'd be furious and he'd lose all the ground he'd gained with her. But if he took her to her apartment, which she shared with Pilar, he was almost certain that she'd politely tell him good-night and send him on his way.

The obvious solution would be to ask her where she wanted to go, but he was afraid if the decision was left to her, all her uncertainties about him would surface and she'd withdraw into her shell again.

They were stopped by a red light, and the turnoff to her apartment was just two blocks ahead. He'd run out of time for musing.

Taking a deep breath, he looked at her. "Will you go to the hotel with me?" He heard the pleading in his tone but hoped that she hadn't. He wanted her to come willingly, because she wanted it as much as he, or not at all.

Her grasp on his thigh tightened momentarily, then loosened, but she didn't answer immediately. When the light changed, he eased the car forward as the seconds seemed to drag by, and beads of sweat broke out on his forehead.

Finally she turned to meet his glance. "Yes," she murmured, so softly that he had to strain to hear. "I want to go home with you."

He was overwhelmed with relief, and it was only then that he realized his fingers were digging into her leg.

A wave of regret swept over him and he instantly released her and wrapped his hand around the steering wheel. "Oh, damn, sweetheart, I'm sorry. I wasn't aware...I mean, I never meant to hurt you, or to influence you—"

"You didn't," she said as she rubbed her palm in a more sweeping caress of his thigh, sending his nerves into spasms, "but I'm glad it was that important to you."

Placing his hand over hers, he picked it up and kissed it, then put it in her lap. "Brace yourself, honey. I've just run out of both patience and control."

He stepped on the gas and drove the mile or so to the hotel as fast as he safely could. Once there, he handed the car over to the parking attendant and escorted Elizabeth across the lobby to the bank of elevators. They were the only ones waiting, and when the lift arrived it was empty.

They entered, and as soon as the doors closed they were in each other's arms. Deny wasn't sure which of them had reached out first, but it didn't matter. She tipped her face up to his and their mouths fused as he widened his stance to press her close between his thighs in an effort to relieve some of the pressure that was driving him crazy.

He'd been having that problem ever since he'd wakened from his nap that afternoon with her snuggled against him, their legs and arms entwined. The shower had helped, but his passion for her was hard to control. She was so desirable all the way from her mop of red curls to those tiny feet that were so kissable, and he loved her to distraction.

The elevator stopped, and they sprang apart just before the doors opened to admit several more passengers.

He'd managed to calm down a little by the time they got to his suite, and as he unlocked the door and ushered her into the living room he told himself he wasn't going to rush this. In spite of his overactive hormones he wasn't after a quick roll between the sheets. He wanted to make their most intimate coming together special for her, an act of love that would show her how much he wanted and needed her, not just for a few hours but for the rest of their lives.

He had the whole night to convince her that she needed him, as well. That he would cherish her and never again let her down, and he wasn't going to ruin it by ravishing her the minute the door closed behind them.

He closed his eyes and offered up a quick, fervent prayer for strength.

Elizabeth silently cursed the sudden attack of nervousness that had overtaken her as they walked down the hall toward Deny's suite. Just seconds before, they'd shared a totally uninhibited embrace in a public elevator, but now, as she looked around the familiar room, her stomach roiled and her hands shook.

The first thing she noticed was that the bed she and Deny had slept on was gone, tucked back into its hiding place in the wall. He'd brought her in here instead of the bedroom, so he apparently didn't plan to throw her down on the bed and take her immediately.

The idea was ridiculous and she knew it, and even if he did she certainly couldn't blame him. Their restrained foreplay had been going on since late afternoon, and she'd been as hot and eager as he, so why was she chickening out now?

Chickening out? No! Never. The very thought was reprehensible. She wouldn't do that to him. He'd given her a choice, and she'd chosen to spend the night with him. In doing so she knowingly agreed to all of that decision's ramifications. She wasn't a tease. She couldn't, wouldn't, back out now.

Her heart was pounding with anxiety, and when he put his hand on her shoulder, she jumped. "I didn't mean to startle you," he said. "I asked if you wanted me to take your wrap, but you didn't answer."

When they'd left the train, she'd put on her black velvet jacket to ward off the chilly night breeze from the bay. "Oh. Yes, please," she said as she undid the single button at her throat and let him slide the garment off her arms.

"Would you like a drink? We have a fully stocked bar." He took off his blazer and hung it, and her jacket, in the closet.

"Maybe a glass of sparkling water if you have it." She had to be alone for a moment to pull herself together. "Um...may I use your bathroom?"

"Right over there." He pointed to a door on the inside wall.

He headed for the bar, and she went into the bathroom and shut the door, then leaned back against it and closed her eyes.

What was the matter with her anyway? She was behaving like a wide-eyed schoolgirl on her first date. This was Deny, the man she probably knew better than he knew himself. She couldn't be afraid of him....

Oh, but she was, and with good reason. What she was about to commit herself to was against all the values she'd been brought up with. Something she wasn't sure she could live with, although she had to try because the alternative was too painful to endure.

Loving Deny came easy, too easy. But trusting him didn't. She wasn't sure she ever would, so she had just two choices. She could give in to the loving and gamble that he wouldn't walk away from her again, or she could leave immediately with her virtue intact and never look back.

She grimaced. *Yeah. Sure. You could also fly to the moon if you had wings. But you don't have and never will. Neither do you have the ability to put Deny out of your life and forget him. It would be easier to grow wings, so quit your sniveling and behave like a woman. Go out there and claim your man, and be prepared to pay the price.*

A few minutes later Elizabeth returned to the living room. Deny was standing at the window with his back to her. He turned and she saw that he had a glass in both hands.

Although he smiled, she could see the strain behind it as he walked toward her. "Here's your drink. Shall we sit down?"

He handed her one of the glasses and they sat side by side on the long, curved sofa. She'd come to terms with her decision, and she was much calmer as she lifted the fizzy water to her mouth and felt it tickle her nose as she sipped.

Deny's smile had disappeared, and he twirled his glass absently between his palms before finally setting it down on the coffee table. "Elizabeth." His voice shook slightly and he cleared his throat without looking at her. "Honey, if you've changed your mind, just say so. I want you to be sure about this."

Slowly she put down her glass and turned to him. He looked confused and miserable, and she was ashamed of herself for causing him even a moment's doubt.

Lifting her hand, she stroked the lines of tension around his mouth. "Deny, my darling, I haven't changed my mind," she said softly. "I want you. I want your kisses." She leaned over and planted a soft kiss on either side of his lips.

"And I want your caress." She took his hand and put it on the fullness of her breast, then shivered with pleasure as his fingers closed around it and his other arm encircled her waist to pull her close.

"And when we are so ready that we can no longer wait, I want you to become a part of me...." Her words were cut off when his mouth covered hers and his tongue coaxed her lips apart.

Chapter Nine

Elizabeth was lost in erotic sensations. At one time she'd taken Deny's kisses for granted, a mistake she could only blame on her youth and inexperience. She'd thought the supply was inexhaustible. When they were no longer available, she'd missed them with an insatiable craving, and now that she was back in his arms, his hand kneading her breast and his tongue reunited with hers in a slow dance of love, all of her senses seemed heightened and her yearning intensified.

She wasn't aware when he unzipped her dress, but then he raised his head and repositioned her arms so he could slide it off her shoulders. The silken material pooled at her waist, and he unfastened her lacy bra and removed it.

His heated gaze roamed over her nakedness, and she felt both exhilarated and shy. Deny was the only male who'd ever seen her like this, and that was so long ago. He'd been the boy she'd grown up with, the boy she was going to marry then, but now he was a man and driven by desire. She could see it in his eyes and feel it in his touch, and it frightened her a little.

Would she be able to meet his needs? She obviously hadn't been woman enough to three years ago.

Her doubts were banished when he leaned down and took her nipple in his mouth, sending hot blood pulsing through her veins and setting her body on fire. She clasped her arms around his neck, knowing that she was as aroused as he, and that whatever he wanted, she could and would give.

His questing hand roamed over her leg, pushing up the snug skirt until it could go no further because she was sitting on it. Again he raised his head. "I'm afraid you'll have to stand up so I can get that dress off," he said huskily, then went back to nuzzling her breast.

"Maybe we should move into the bedroom," she suggested, wanting to lie with him on the bed but hating to stop what they were doing in order to get there.

"I think that's a great idea." His tone was gravelly with impatience as he stood and pulled her up with him.

Elizabeth slid her dress over her head and carried it with her as they hurried across the hall to the bedroom. Deny threw back the covers while she stepped out of her pumps and removed her panty hose.

He had reached up to loosen the knot of his tie, but his hands stilled as he watched her amble slowly toward him, clad only in silk-and-lace bikini panties. He drew in a ragged breath when she reached out and gently brushed his hands aside and tackled the tie herself.

"My turn," she said, and kissed him on the chin.

She undid the knot and tossed the tie onto the dresser, then started unbuttoning his shirt. The buttons were small and he squirmed impatiently as she worked to push them through the equally small buttonholes.

"Sweetheart, you're driving me crazy," he groaned as he put his hands on her buttocks and pushed her against him.

It was abundantly obvious that he was indeed on the brink of losing control, and she hurried to finish undressing him. When she came to the fly of his slacks, he took over and stripped to his briefs while she climbed into bed.

He followed almost immediately and took her in his arms, but she could feel the fierce tension in him as he fought for restraint. "Everything's happening too quickly," he said, his voice hoarse with desire and frustration. "I don't want it to be over so soon. Let's try to slow down and make it last."

Even as he spoke of holding back, he rolled partially onto her, and his throbbing hardness pressed into her hip.

"Sounds good," she murmured unsteadily as her tongue played with his earlobe, "but how do you suggest we go about that?"

If he wanted to prolong this exquisite torture he'd have to find a way to do it. She was past the ability to think straight.

"I don't think it's possible!" His voice was ragged, but with a quick, almost rough, movement he rolled away from her and lay silently gasping for breath.

She was breathing heavily, too, as she turned onto her side and propped her head up to look at him. He had a magnificent body. Unable to resist, she reached out and ran her finger slowly down the middle of his chest.

When she got to his navel, he captured her hand and brought it to his lips. "You're not a bit of help," he grumbled as he kissed each of her fingers.

"Sorry," she murmured happily and leaned down to take his flat nipple in her mouth.

He uttered an unintelligible oath and his arms came around her like bands of steel, pulling her on top of him.

"You little devil," he rasped. "You're going to make slowing down as difficult for me as you can, aren't you."

She stretched out full length on his hard body and smiled. "Darn right. I like the idea of you not always being in control."

He reared his head up and looked at her with amazement. "Me? In control? When have I ever been in control of myself when you're around? Just touching you sets me on fire and turns my mind to mush."

He laid his head back down and rubbed his hands over her bare back before settling them on her buttocks. "With you for a wife I'll be a burned-out shell before our fifth wedding anniversary."

Elizabeth blinked, and her heart seemed to stop beating. "Wife?" She wasn't aware of speaking, but the word hung suspended in the air.

He grinned. "That *is* what the female marriage partner is still called, isn't it? Or have they come up with a nonsexist term for that relationship now, too? And speaking of marriage, I can arrange to have our blood tests tomorrow. Then we can have the ceremony whenever you want."

Elizabeth felt as if the breath had been knocked out of her. The room seemed to tilt as she sat up and climbed off him before he could grab her. "There's never going to be a wedding ceremony, Deny," she said with cool deliberation as she knelt beside him on the bed. "I'm not going to marry you."

For a moment he just stared at her with a stunned expression. Then he pushed himself up to a sitting position. "What do you mean you're not going to marry me?" His tone was harsh with uncertainty. "If you're teasing me, Elizabeth, it's not funny."

He was deadly serious, and she hurried to explain. "I'm not teasing. It's just that the subject of marriage never came up. If you'd asked me, I'd have told you that I have no intention of marrying you or anyone else."

His expression lightened. "Oh, now I get it. You're mad because I haven't proposed to you again. I'm sorry, honey, but every time I tried, you cut me off and wouldn't listen...."

"No, you still don't understand." This was going to be more difficult than she'd imagined. "I never expected you to propose, otherwise I'd have told you—"

"Told me what, dammit?" The uncertainty in his tone was gone, replaced with anger. "If you don't want to marry me, why are you so willing to make love with me?"

"Because I want you," she snapped, her own anger heating up. "Isn't that reason enough? It's the excuse men have been giving women since the beginning of time when *they* want sex without marriage...."

Elizabeth stopped, appalled by what she'd said. Somehow the words had come out all wrong and sounded hard and uncaring, but before she could back down, Deny practically threw himself off the bed, then turned around and glared at her. "You mean you were just needy and any man would do?" he thundered. "You wanted a stud and I was available?" His face was white with rage.

"No!" She pulled the sheet up to cover her nakedness. "Damn you, Deny, if you'd listen to me calmly instead of breathing fire and smoke and beating your chest with righteous indignation I'd..."

"Calmly!" By now they were shouting at each other. "How in hell can I be calm when you've got me so tied in knots that I'm suffocating?"

He picked up his trousers and started to put them on as he continued to rant. "This is your way of getting back at me for canceling the wedding, isn't it? Revenge! God, how sweet it must be. Get me so aroused that I'm about to explode, then coldly make it impossible to complete the act."

Zipping up his fly, he reached for his shirt and put it on. "Okay, I'll grant you, I probably deserved it, but I didn't deliberately set out to hurt you."

Before she could deny his assumptions, he stormed over to the telephone and pushed a button, then snarled at whoever answered. "Get me a cab. Immediately. We'll be right down."

Elizabeth was dumbfounded. This had gotten completely out of hand. "Deny..."

"Get dressed," he ordered as he finished buttoning his shirt and tucked it into his pants. "The game is over. You won." He picked up his shoes and stalked out of the room, slamming the door behind him.

She scrambled off the bed and started to follow him, but then remembered she was nude. Her whole body slumped with discouragement as she picked up her clothes and dressed. With her usual clumsiness she'd really made a mess of things this time.

It wouldn't do any good to try to reason with him tonight. He wasn't in any mood to listen. Tomorrow, after he'd had a chance to cool down, she'd catch up with him and force him to let her explain.

Deny was waiting for her when she entered the living room. He didn't speak, just took her arm and led her out of the suite and down the hall where an elevator was just opening its doors. He ushered her inside and they silently rode to the lobby.

There was a cab waiting at the front curb. The doorman helped her into the back seat while Deny gave the driver the address of her apartment and handed him a bill. She expected him to get into the taxi with her, but instead he just leaned down to look at her and said, "Goodbye, Elizabeth," before shutting the door.

It was several blocks before her mind cleared enough to realize that he hadn't said good-night. He'd said *goodbye*.

Elizabeth had had nightmares during her lifetime, but never before when she was awake.

Not that she hadn't tried to sleep, she had, but her mind was on rewind. It kept replaying that hour at Deny's apartment over and over again. Except for when it was on fast forward and dredged up worst-case scenarios such as the possibility of his flying back to Washington and refusing to take calls or messages from her.

The awful thing about that was that it would serve her right. It's what she'd done to him three and a half years ago.

Finally, at five o'clock, she got up even though today was her second day off and she didn't have to go to work. She had to track Deny down, and if he'd spent as miserable a night as she had, he wasn't going to welcome her.

She couldn't bear the knowledge that he thought she'd planned retribution and had deliberately set him up for a fall. Even when she'd been the most bitter she'd never have done a thing like that.

She raced against the clock to be through in the bathroom and dressed in a knee-length blue plaid pleated skirt and a blue cardigan over a cream silk blouse by the time Pilar's alarm went off. Her apartment mate would want to hear all about the excursion yesterday, and Elizabeth wasn't up to talking about anything until she'd straightened out her misunderstanding with Deny.

By the time Pilar was up and dressed, Elizabeth had the coffee made for her and escaped with a hasty goodbye and the promise that she'd tell her about the trip to Napa Valley later.

"Yeah, sure," Pilar called after her. "And maybe you'll also explain where the hell you're going all dressed up at five-thirty in the morning?"

Elizabeth chuckled and waved, then shut the door behind her.

Deny sat slumped on the sofa, staring at the grainy black-and-white images on television as the vintage movie reached a noisy climax and jarred him out of his drowsy doldrums. He was bone tired, but his hyperactive mind wouldn't let him sleep.

After sending Elizabeth home in the cab, he'd walked. Blocks, miles, he wasn't sure how many, but it hadn't helped. He'd been too keyed up to even notice that the breeze off the bay was cold and he was wearing only a thin shirt, trousers and shoes, until his teeth started chattering.

When he'd returned to the hotel, he'd undressed and gone to bed, mostly to get warm, but also hoping to at least rest if not sleep. It had been a hopeless desire, like all the other desires he'd felt tonight, and eventually he'd gotten up, put on a heavy toweling robe and turned on the television.

Even that had been useless. He couldn't concentrate on what was on the screen. All he could see and hear was the picture of Elizabeth that was embedded in his mind as she knelt beside him on the bed, wearing nothing but a scrap of pantie, and told him she had no intention of marrying him, ever. That she just wanted him for a few nights of passion before he left town again!

He shuddered and rubbed his hands over his face. No, that wasn't exactly true. He'd rattled her when that damn quick temper of his exploded, and then he'd compounded his many mistakes by refusing to give her a chance to explain just what she had meant.

After all, he had only himself to blame for the tangled mess he'd made of his life. He'd called Elizabeth immature years ago when she wouldn't move to Washington with him. Now he realized that he'd been no more mature than she was, and he'd been three years older.

Apparently he still hadn't caught up with her in that department. Even after all this time, he was still rushing things, acting on impulse instead of listening to his own instincts. He'd known she needed time to accept him again, even as a friend, but he'd let his hormones rule his head and all his good intentions had gone up in smoke along with his self-control.

Was he chasing an impossible dream? Did she—

The insistent noise he'd been hearing finally broke through his troubled thoughts, and he realized that someone was banging on his door. He sat up and looked at his watch. Not quite six o'clock. It was still dark outside.

He stood and walked to the door in the enclosed front hall that connected the two rooms. "Who is it? What do you want?"

"It's Elizabeth," called the voice from the other side. "Please let me in."

With an exclamation of surprise, he unlocked the door and opened it. Elizabeth stood there, looking small and unsure and incredibly beautiful even though her makeup didn't entirely hide the dark circles under her ravaged blue eyes. He wasn't sure whether he should let her in or send her away, but he'd sent her away last night and he'd been roasting in hell ever since. He wasn't going to put himself through that again.

She stood quietly, seeming to know his thoughts and waiting for his decision. "Come in," was all he managed to say as he stepped aside to allow her to enter.

Elizabeth breathed a sigh of relief as she preceded Deny into the living room. When he'd taken so long to answer her knock, she'd been terrified that he'd checked out and gone back to Washington.

Instead he must have been asleep. At least he looked like he'd just gotten out of bed and slipped into his robe and slippers. His hair was tousled and he had a dark stubble of beard, but he didn't look rested. His eyes were shadowed, and his expression was grim.

"I have to talk to you," she said as she stopped in the middle of the room and turned to look at him.

He nodded. "I know, but let me get dressed first. Why don't you call room service and order breakfast with plenty of coffee while I shower and shave? It won't take me but a few minutes."

His voice had a hollow sound, and he really did look awful. "Yes. All right, I'll do that," she said, but when he started to turn away, she put her hand on his arm to stop him. "Deny, you don't look well. Are you feeling all right?" Her tone was low and filled with concern.

He shook his head slowly. "Not really. Are you?"

"No. I didn't sleep. I'm sorry if I woke you."

"You didn't. I haven't slept, either. I put on the robe and slippers because I was cold."

Her fingers tightened on his arm. "Then you'd better take a long, hot shower."

He reached out and brushed a strand of hair off her cheek. "I will."

He turned and went into the bedroom.

Elizabeth called room service, then went to stand at the huge picture window that looked out over the city from the eighteenth floor. The dark sky was turning gray although the stream of cars on the streets below still had their lights on.

Oakland was back to business as usual, and only the poor souls who had been burned out or lost loved ones were still incapacitated by the holocaust that had leveled a goodly portion of the city just days before.

She sighed and turned away. No, that wasn't fair. The fire storm had touched nearly everyone living in the area, if not personally then through friends, and it would be years before the horror dimmed. Meanwhile, life went on, and the survivors who were smart put the pain and loss behind them and moved with the flow. Anything else was emotional suicide.

So why couldn't she forget her past trauma and get on with her future?

Because she wasn't smart, that's why. She was a flawed human being like so many others who couldn't shrug off the anguish, or forget the betrayal, even though she still loved the betrayer.

Instead she was prepared to compromise. Deny might be disappointed when she told him what she had in mind, but surely he'd eventually agree to her terms. If he truly loved her, he'd want to be with her under any conditions. Wouldn't he?

A flurry of activity coming from the television distracted her, and she glanced at the set on the bar. It was the early-morning news program on one of the local stations, and she sat down on the couch and relaxed against the soft upholstery. She might as well watch it. Maybe it would take her mind off her own problems.

Fifteen minutes later the bell captain arrived with their breakfast, and he'd just left when Deny came back from the bedroom, showered, shaved and dressed in jeans and a navy blue sweatshirt. He looked better, but there was no happiness in his expression, only despair.

The server had set the food on the table, and when they were seated, Deny lifted the cover of the dish in front of him. It was a bowl of oatmeal, and for just a moment his sadness lifted and he smiled. "You remembered." He seemed genuinely pleased. "And you even ordered brown sugar for it."

Elizabeth smiled, too. "Of course I did. Did you really think I'd forget?"

Deny's mother was a firm believer in the nutritional value of oatmeal, and served it hot and smothered in cream every morning without fail while her children were growing up. They'd been expected to eat every mouthful of it, and no excuses were accepted. A couple of his brothers grew to hate it, but Deny didn't consider that the day had started until he had his oatmeal with brown sugar.

"Yes, I did," he said, the smile gone as quickly as it had appeared. "You seem to have forgotten so many other things about me."

She shook her head sadly. "No, Deny, I haven't forgotten anything where you're concerned, although, God knows, I tried. Now, please, let's finish eating before we talk."

They watched the news and finished their breakfast in silence, then took their coffee cups and moved to the sofa. Deny picked up the remote control and turned off the television, then drained his cup and put it on the coffee table.

He didn't look at her as he spoke. "Elizabeth, I'm sorry I behaved like such a bastard last night. I ranted and raved and didn't give you a chance to speak at all."

She put her cup down, also. "I understand. I'd have done the same thing if our positions had been reversed. I honestly didn't know that by agreeing to spend the night here you thought I expected you to marry me."

He ran his hand through his hair. "What else would I think? You're not the type for one-night stands...."

He stopped and looked at her, and she saw the unspoken question in his startled expression. *Are you?*

"No, I'm not," she said. "In my whole life there's never been another man I wanted to make love with, only you. That's why I was so willing. I'm sorry you misunderstood and thought I was just using you."

Deny's expression changed to one of confusion. "I must be missing something here. If you care enough about me to sleep with me, then why won't you marry me?"

Elizabeth knew he wouldn't accept an evasive answer. She'd have to override her pride and tell him just how deeply he'd wounded her. She gathered her thoughts and spoke slowly, weighing her words to make sure they meant what she wanted to say.

"There are two reasons why I won't marry you, Deny. Both equally compelling. I can't trust you, and after what I went through in canceling our wedding, I could never face the prospect of planning another one."

She closed her eyes and forced herself to relive those agonizing memories as she told him how shattered she'd been when he broke their engagement, how heartbreaking and humiliating it was for her to cancel the wedding so publicly. "I sent telegrams to those invited, put a notice in the newspaper telling about the cancellation, and then sat down and wrote personal notes explaining the situation, which were sent with each of the returned gifts."

The scenes replaying in her mind were too painful, and she opened her eyes, hoping to dislodge them. "You can't imagine how emotionally and physically damaging the pity of all those people was. I felt discarded, like I'd been used up and thrown away. Everybody was talking about it and speculating on what happened. I threw up almost everything I tried to eat and lost ten pounds.''

She paused and noticed that Deny's face was white, his expression grim. "Why didn't someone tell me?" he moaned. "I spent that summer in a fog of regret and loneliness, knowing I'd made a colossal mistake but unable to fix it. You wouldn't accept my calls or letters, my own family was barely speaking to me, and I missed you so much I didn't know how I could find the strength to go on. If I'd known you were suffering, too, I'd have come back and made you listen to me.''

Elizabeth shook her head sadly. "It wouldn't have done any good, and would only have made things worse. Mother finally took me on a cruise of the Caribbean Islands, and being far away from Oakland, as well as the enforced rest and the sea breeze, did help. Shortly after we returned, I went back to school and didn't come home again for two years.''

Deny looked sick, and she regretted the necessity to unload her emotional garbage on him after all this time. He'd apologized for the agony he'd caused her, and she got no satisfaction out of punishing him like this, but it was the only way she could make him understand what she was going to propose.

"Elizabeth, if there's anything I can do to make up for the pain I've caused you, I will." His voice was low and filled with regret. "I love you. I always have, but at the time I thought it would have been a mistake for us to marry so young. I bungled it badly, but does that mean I have to pay for it all the rest of my life?''

He still didn't understand. "I'm not making you pay for anything, Deny," she said softly. "It's just that you broke something much more important than my pride. You killed my trust, and even if I could face the prospects of another marriage ceremony, I can't marry a man I can't trust."

He sighed and stood up, then looked down at her. "Sweetheart, you've known me all your life. Did I ever let you down before that? Until that day had I ever not been there for you when you needed a friend? A big brother? A lover?"

Tears pooled in Elizabeth's eyes as she shook her head. "No, never. You were always there for me."

He rubbed his own eyes with his knuckles, and she wondered if he was fighting tears, too. "Then am I not to be allowed even one transgression, horrendous though it was? Don't you have any faith in me at all? I swear with God as my witness that I'll never leave you or let you down again."

Elizabeth wanted to believe him, actually she did believe him, and maybe eventually she could put aside her fear of rejection and trust him again, but there was still a stumbling block, and one that would never go away.

"Maybe I am being unreasonable on that point," she admitted, "but even if I could learn to trust you again I still couldn't marry you. I have an actual psychological block where weddings are concerned. I can't even attend someone else's, let alone plan my own."

His expression lightened a little. "We don't have to have a big one. Just a simple ceremony with our families present."

It sounded so reasonable, but even the thought of that brought a wave of nausea. Ruefully she shook her head. "Even that is impossible. There would still be preparations that had to be made, arrange for the church, the priest, plan the reception, buy wedding clothes..."

She shuddered, then bent over and covered her face with her hands. "Oh God, I'll never buy another wedding gown as long as I live!" It was a cry of repulsion.

"Elizabeth!" Deny sat down beside her again and put his arm across her shoulders. "Honey, it's all right."

She straightened up and he took her in his arms and held her with her head against his chest. His heart was racing and she knew he was frightened for her.

"You see what I mean?" she murmured. "Just talking about a wedding throws me into a sick panic. I'll never marry anyone!"

Much as she loved the warm security of his embrace, she forced herself to push away and sit up. She didn't want to send him mixed messages. He had to understand that a wedding was out of the question.

"Dammit, Elizabeth, you love me," he said roughly. "And don't deny it. You wouldn't be willing to make love with me if you didn't. Your strong moral standards wouldn't allow it. You can protest all you want, but you love me and I love you and that's a given."

She knew it was useless to deny it. "You're right," she admitted. "I do love you, but you're wrong about the flexibility of my moral standards."

She paused, then took a deep breath and continued. "I won't marry you, but if you want me to, I will live with you."

Deny's eyes widened, and he looked as if she'd knocked the breath out of him. "What!" It was a yip of surprise and disbelief.

He was reacting the way she'd expected. "I said if you still want me to I'll quit my job here in Oakland and live with you in Washington, but there will be no commitment. That way when one or both of us want out, we can just walk away with no fuss and no publicity."

He looked as if he'd been poleaxed, and when he spoke he sounded like it, too. "Are you telling me that you want to be my mistress!"

That raised her ire. "Not your mistress, no. That would mean you were supporting me, and I don't need any man to take care of me. I'm saying we can be equal partners sharing a living arrangement as lovers."

"And what about the family we always planned on having? Whose name will they have? Mine? Yours? Or one of those hyphenated mixtures?"

He was trying to get a rise out of her, but the question of a family was a crucial one, one she'd agonized over, and she answered him in all seriousness. "I'm afraid that dream will have to be scrapped. I won't bring children into the world unless I'm married."

Deny couldn't believe what he was hearing. His sweet, innocent little Elizabeth, raised with all the moral restrictions of the church, who wouldn't let him put his hand under her skirt until they were formally engaged, was suggesting that they live together without vows, commitment or babies. And, even more preposterous, with the agreement that either of them was free to walk away from the arrangement at any time with no ties or regrets.

Oh, my darling, what have I done to you.

It was a monstrous idea, and still if it was the only way he could have her he was cruelly tempted. He wanted her so badly that he'd take her under any other term...but not that one.

"Elizabeth, I don't believe you understand all the ramifications of what you're suggesting." He managed to keep his tone calm and reasonably impersonal. "We've been raised to believe that the vows of marriage are sacred and binding."

She nodded. "I know. That's why I won't speak them with you. I don't want you bound to me if you decide at some later date that you want to be free again."

He bit back an oath. Obviously that had been the wrong tactic.

He tried again. "I'm not going to want to be free of you whether we're married of not, but think of our parents. They would feel upset and ashamed if we lived together without getting married, and they don't deserve that."

Tears welled in her beautiful eyes and ran down her cheeks, and he felt like a heel. Dammit, he hadn't meant to make her cry!

"Do you think I haven't thought of that?" she said on a sob. "It tears me apart to think of doing that to them, but we'd be clear across the country. No one around here would have to know."

Obviously she'd thought this out well. She had answers for all of his objections. "Maybe not, but that wouldn't lessen their heartbreak over their son and daughter behaving so contrary to all their deeply held beliefs. Elizabeth, think about it."

She glared at him, and there were bright spots of anger on her white cheeks. "I have thought about it," she said tightly. "Do you think this is something I just decided on the spur of the moment?"

Her gaze held his for a moment then wavered. "I love you, Deny, but I can't marry you. I know I'm being selfish, but if you love me and want me it will have to be on my terms."

A sob shook her. "Or maybe I'm assuming too much. Maybe you don't want me under those conditions."

She looked so young and so small and so unhappy, and his arms ached to hold her, but he knew if he did he'd cave in and agree to anything she asked if she'd just come with him and be his love. Instead, he tried one more time to tell her how wrong that would be.

"Elizabeth, I want you so much that I'd agree to almost any conditions to keep you with me, but you're asking me to go along with a plan that would destroy you, and that's something I cannot do."

Her eyes widened and she opened her mouth to protest, but he didn't give her a chance to speak. "I know you too well. You'd always feel guilty living with me outside the vows of the church, and it would mean we'd never have the babies you've always wanted. Eventually you'd grow to hate me, and yourself, as well. I couldn't do that to either of us. I've already hurt you far too deeply, I'm not going to compound it with still another mistake in judgment."

She hung her head then, like a child who has been reprimanded. "You're probably right," she said, her tone ragged with emotion. "I've worked hard on convincing myself I could be happy living that way if it meant being with you, but there are so many others who would be hurt...."

A wave of pain nearly blinded him. How could he let her go? It was like tearing out his heart. How could he say goodbye to the person who was dearer to him than anyone else in his life?

On the other hand, how could he live with her in a way that was contrary to everything they'd been taught and watch her sweet innocence slowly fade as her soul became more and more burdened with guilt, which it surely would?

It was time to put an end to this torment they were inflicting on each other. He steeled himself to get through the next few minutes.

"Then there really isn't anything else for us to talk about, is there?" He regretted the coolness of his voice, but it was either that or break down and cry with her.

She raised her head to look at him, and he saw the anguish in her eyes. "No, I guess there isn't. I . . . I'd better be leaving."

She stood and he rose with her and watched as she moved away from him. She picked up her purse then paused and turned to him. "Deny...will you...will you kiss me good-bye?"

His fists clenched at his sides and he drew in a tortured breath. "No, Elizabeth. Please—don't ask that of me." He knew that if he touched her he'd never let her go.

With a strangled sob she turned and left.

Chapter Ten

During the next two and a half weeks, Elizabeth learned to hate her dainty, obscenely expensive, crystal alarm clock, a gift from her parents when she'd left home for college five years before. Its bell-like tones awakened her too soon once she'd finally fallen asleep after still another night of rolling and tossing in her single bed.

The seventeen days since she'd walked out of Deny's hotel room, and his life, had been bearable only because she was kept so busy at the hospital, as well as with the mountain of work, both physical and legal, that had been required to put her parents' fire loss in perspective and get them settled temporarily in a hotel suite after their return to Oakland a week earlier.

That in itself had been a horrendous ordeal. Although they'd read the newspaper accounts, seen the pictures and had time to absorb the fact of their catastrophe, when confronted with the actual sight of the disaster, it was a shattering experience.

Even so, all the activity only served to dull the pain of losing Deny a second time, but at night it returned full-blown in restless sleep and tormenting nightmares.

She was firmly convinced that it was Pilar, with her gentle insistence that Elizabeth talk with her about her feelings, that kept her sane. Pilar was her safety valve, the only person close to her that she could talk to about her second breakup with Deny without endangering the newly cemented friendship between the Kelly and the O'Halloran families. Both parties needed that deep, special relationship in order to cope with the tragic losses they'd suffered in the fire storm.

Elizabeth and Deny had managed to convince both of their families that they had made up their differences and were now good friends, so their parents could resume their longtime bond without having to take sides in a feud between their children. Which left only Pilar to probe Elizabeth's pain and persuade her to voice it as a means of dealing with it.

"You have to get it out in the open," Pilar had wisely said. "Three years ago you made the mistake of holding everything in and refusing to acknowledge the pain. It festered and couldn't heal. Don't make that same mistake this time, Liz. If you don't want to talk to me then get counseling, but talk to somebody and work through the anguish."

Although exposing her heartbreak to anyone was distasteful to Elizabeth, there was nobody she would trust more than Pilar to keep her secrets inviolate. Talking to her had been Elizabeth's salvation, not only in sharing the burden of her grief, but in helping her view the situation from both sides.

On this Sunday evening in the middle of November, Pilar played the devil's advocate, taking Deny's side in an effort to force Elizabeth to better understand his point of view. "If it had been you who was unsure of your feelings for Deny three years ago, would you have married him anyway?'' she asked.

''Probably not,'' Elizabeth answered, somewhat shaken. ''But I wouldn't have waited until a week before the wedding to call it off.''

''You mean you'd have known exactly how you felt?'' Pilar continued. ''You wouldn't have had any doubts? You wouldn't have hesitated for fear of hurting Deny or your parents, who had been planning the big expensive wedding?''

''No. I mean yes.'' Elizabeth was thoroughly confused. ''I mean it didn't happen like that.''

''It did for Deny,'' Pilar said mercilessly. ''Doesn't the fact that he couldn't bear to hurt you count for anything?''

Elizabeth's head started to spin as her temper escalated. ''Of course it does, but—''

''But you've never been wrong, or made a mistake. Is that what you're saying?''

What was the matter with her friend? Elizabeth thought. Why was she acting as if Deny were the wronged person. ''Dammit, Pilar, whose side are you on?''

''I'm not taking sides,'' Pilar said calmly. ''I just want you to make a fully informed, well-thought-out decision this time. One you can live with, and you can't do that unless you try to understand Deny's reasoning. Ask yourself a few important questions, such as what kind of person is he? How often had he broken his promises or lied to you before the wedding crisis? Did he ever mistreat you in any way? Do you honestly think that he can't ever again be trusted? Or is this your way of protecting yourself—or getting even with him?''

''That's a rotten thing to say,'' Elizabeth snapped. ''How can I trust him again after what he did to me?''

Pilar held up her hand for silence. ''Don't answer, just listen. These are questions for you to wrestle with privately. But there's one more that is most important of all. Are you better off without him than you'd be with him? Forget about your pride, and think it through carefully, Liz. You're at a turning point that will determine all the rest of your life.''

They changed the subject then as they worked together to clean up the kitchen after the evening meal, but the questions lingered in Elizabeth's mind.

What kind of person was Deny during the years they were together?

That one was easy. He was her best friend. He laughed with her, cried with her, protected her when she needed protecting, made excuses for her when she did something wrong. He'd been everything she'd ever wanted in a playmate, friend and, later, a lover.

How often had he broken promises or lied to her?

Never. That is, not up to the time he told her he loved her and promised to marry her, but his lies and deceit then more than overbalanced his earlier integrity.

Had he ever mistreated her?

No! She couldn't even conceive of him doing such a thing. Deny was a kind and gentle man. He went out of his way to keep from hurting anyone.

So why couldn't she ever trust him again?

That question was more difficult. It touched her very core. She'd trusted him totally once and he'd betrayed that faith. How could she be sure he wouldn't do it again?

Was she punishing him?

Absolutely not. She'd never do a thing like that. He had forfeited her trust, but she wasn't vindictive. She just wanted to protect herself from being destroyed the next time he let her down.

As for the last question, she skirted it altogether. She didn't even want to think about it.

For two days the questions badgered her, disturbing her sleep, and interfered with her concentration at work. She pushed them away only to have them reappear, demanding to be answered. Not superficial answers but soul-searching ones.

The last two were the ones that nearly drove her out of her mind.

Did she truly believe he could never be trusted again? Was she better off without him than she would be with him?

There was no objective answer to the question of his reliability, it was too subjective. But she was finally forced to face the fact that she loved the man without surcease, no matter what he'd done to her in the past, or what he may do to her in the future. Therefore she'd be better off with him than she would be without him. Wouldn't she?

Besides, what sin had he committed that was so unforgivable?

So he made a mistake, a big one, but who hasn't? Hadn't she made one just as big when she'd sent him away this last time. For twenty years Deny was there for her. He only let her down once. Wasn't everybody entitled to one mistake?

And who made her God to pass judgment on others? She was anything but perfect. She'd been too blind to see it before, but she'd failed him twice. The first time was when he wanted her to move to Washington with him once they were married. She'd been too immature to consider how much the position Deny'd been offered meant to him at that time.

Was it possible that the psychological block she had against weddings had been subconsciously erected so she wouldn't have to accept the possibility that she was as much to blame for their aborted ceremony as he was?

She was trying to protect herself from the possibility of future pain, but pain wasn't a possibility, it was a probability. A fact of life that everyone had to deal with. The only way to be assured of no more pain was to die, and Elizabeth wanted to live, fully and completely. To revel in the joys and learn to manage the tragedies.

She also knew that such a life was not possible for her without Deny to share it, so she'd darn well better stop playing the role of jilted maiden and claim him. She wasn't likely to get a third chance.

That night, for the first time in three weeks, she fell asleep as soon as she crawled into bed and slept a full eight hours before she woke up feeling rested and absolutely certain of what she was going to do.

However, just the thought of it brought a wave of nausea, and Elizabeth knew she had to put her plans into motion immediately before she was tempted to back out. The first step was to call one of the nurses who owed her compensatory time and arranged for her to work Elizabeth's shift that day. Then she dialed Rosalie's home and asked to talk to Maggie.

"Elizabeth, dear, how sweet of you to call," Maggie said when she answered the telephone.

"Aunt Maggie, I must see you alone right away. May I come over or do you have other plans for this morning?"

"Why, yes, of course you may come over. Is something wrong?"

"No, nothing's wrong," Elizabeth hastened to assure her. "Actually, I hope everything is finally going to be right, but I need your help."

She knew she was only confusing the poor woman further, but she couldn't take the time to get her thoughts in proper order.

"You know I'll do whatever I can," Maggie said in a puzzled tone. "Come anytime. I'll be waiting for you."

The early-morning traffic across the Bay Bridge was a snarled mess as usual, but when Elizabeth finally arrived at the house, Maggie met her at the door and took her up to the suite of rooms she and Aidan were using.

"Now, sit down, have something to eat, and tell me what this is all about," Maggie said as she poured coffee from a silver pot into a china cup and handed it to Elizabeth.

Elizabeth took it and sank back into a comfortable chair, but refused the home-baked cinnamon rolls Maggie offered. "Thanks but no, I'd better not. My stomach is pretty queasy."

The older woman's expression changed to one of concern. "Are you ill?"

Elizabeth shook her head. "Not really. My health is fine, but I'll probably be throwing up a lot—"

Maggie looked shocked. "Elizabeth, you're not—"

She paused, and Elizabeth smiled. "Pregnant? No, not yet, but I hope to be soon if everything works out."

"Elizabeth Kelly," Maggie said sternly. "I want you to stop this nonsense and tell me what's going on."

Elizabeth nodded and launched into her story. She told Maggie about how difficult canceling her wedding had been for her, and the severe nausea she'd suffered then and still did at even the thought of a wedding. She went on to admit that she and Deny had quarreled again over her refusal to marry him, and that they had not parted friends as they had led their families to believe.

"We haven't been in touch at all since he went back to Washington, and I've been miserable," Elizabeth finished. "So miserable, in fact, that I've finally come to the realization that I love Deny too much to live without him. I want to marry him, Aunt Maggie, but I still can't face the thought of a wedding. So here's what I have in mind. I need your help, but I don't want anyone else to know what we're planning. Not even Deny."

Maggie listened, wide-eyed with astonishment, while Elizabeth outlined her strategy. When she was through, Maggie was almost, but not quite, speechless. "My dear, I don't know how you can possibly pull that off. At the very least you'll have to tell Deny what you want to do, and what about your parents?"

Elizabeth shook her head. "No. Not Deny, not my parents, not even Aidan. I realize that Deny may not still want me. I won't embarrass him or try to coerce him if he doesn't, but if that happens only he and you and I will know what I wanted of him. I couldn't bear to have anyone else know that I'd been left at the altar twice by the same man. Especially not my parents."

A sob escaped before she could stop it. "Please, Aunt Maggie. I can't do this without your help."

Maggie rose and came to put her arms around Elizabeth and hold her head against her soft bosom. "I'd do almost anything to have you for a daughter-in-law. If that means being part of this wild scheme of yours then count me in. Now, tell me, how am I supposed to convince Deny to come home for Thanksgiving when he's already told us he can't possibly get away again so soon?"

In Washington, D.C., Denis O'Halloran was just walking out of his office on his way to a luncheon meeting when his phone rang. He'd told his secretary he was leaving, so it must be something important for her to have put the call through.

He walked back to his desk and picked up the receiver. "Yes, Helen?"

"You have a call from your mother in Oakland. I know you said you were going out, but—"

"My mother?" His tone was sharp with anxiety. She'd never called him at work before. "Put her on."

There was a click and Maggie spoke. "Denis, I'm sorry to bother you—"

Deny couldn't wait for her to finish. "Mom, what's the matter? Are you all right? Is it Dad?"

"Denis, calm down. Everything's fine. I just wanted to talk to you about coming home for Thanksgiving. Your father and I want you to come home, dear. I know you're busy, but the whole family will be here and we want you with us."

The nagging anxiety returned. "I explained to you why I can't come. I'm really swamped trying to catch up after being there last time. Mom, are you sure you're all right? You're not keeping something from me, are you?"

There was a long pause at the other end of the line, and his suspicion turned to fear. "Mother, answer me."

"There's nothing wrong with me," she said finally. "I tire rather easily, and sometimes I still have to use the oxygen, but that is to be expected."

"Let me talk to Dad," Deny growled.

"I'm sorry, but he's not here. He still goes into the office three days a week, you know. Look, honey, won't you rearrange your work schedule so you can come home for the holiday? Please. It would mean so much to your father and me."

Deny's resistance melted into his anxiety. It wasn't like his mother to insist on having her own way. Why was it so important to her that he come home again when he'd been there less than a month ago? Was there something she wasn't telling him? He'd better go home and find out for himself.

"Okay, Mom," he heard himself saying. "If it's that important to you I'll fly in Wednesday afternoon. And I want to talk to your doctor. Call him and make an appointment for me to see him."

He hung up a few minutes later and muttered a quiet oath. Damn! It wasn't his work that had kept him from going home for Thanksgiving. That was just the excuse he'd given his parents. It was the fact that Elizabeth was there that kept him away.

How could he go back to Oakland knowing she was so close, so available, and not give in to the temptation to claim her on any terms she wanted? He didn't think he could take much more of the hell he'd been going through since she'd walked out of his hotel room after destroying any hope he'd had of spending the rest of his life with her.

Thanksgiving dawned bright and warm. A beautiful day for what Elizabeth had planned, but her nerves were ragged and although she was hungry, she didn't eat breakfast, because she knew it would just come back up. She'd had that problem off and on all week, and she'd be glad when this day was over, no matter how it turned out.

The Kellys and the O'Hallorans were celebrating the holiday together as had been their custom for as long as Elizabeth could remember until the rift that interrupted their friendship. This year dinner was being held at Rosalie's house in San Francisco since both of the family homes had been destroyed in the fire.

At a little after noon Elizabeth swallowed another dose of a stomach-soothing medication the doctor had prescribed, and dressed in the cream lace cocktail-length dress and matching shoes that she'd selected for the occasion. It was dressier than she would normally wear for an early family dinner, but not enough to cause comment.

She applied makeup a little more liberally than usual in an effort to camouflage the lines of strain around her mouth and the dark circles under her eyes. Her titian hair was too curly to do much with, but she tamed it somewhat by brushing it up and back on the sides and anchoring it with antique mother-of-pearl combs while it cascaded to below her shoulders in back.

A glance at her watch told her it was nearly two and her parents would be there in a few minutes to pick her up for the drive across the bay to Rosalie's. Elizabeth had learned from Maggie that Deny's plan to fly in on Wednesday had fallen through when he was unable to get a booking until Thanksgiving day. His flight was due in at two-fifteen, and he would take a taxi to the house. She wanted to be there when he arrived.

With trembling hands, she checked the contents of the big leather pouch-type shoulder purse she'd packed earlier. By the time she'd assured herself that she had everything she'd need, her parents drove up in the shiny new black foreign car they'd bought to replace the cars that had been destroyed in the fire.

Because of the holiday the Bay Area traffic was a little less gridlocked than usual, but even so Elizabeth had to bite her lip to keep from urging her dad to hurry. The suspense that tormented her had built to an almost unbearable crescendo, but since Connor and Kathleen Kelly knew nothing about their daughter's plans, they were content to take their time and enjoy visiting with her.

Even so, they got there before Deny and were warmly greeted by the many O'Halloran clan members. Elizabeth noticed that the house was adorned with large, beautiful floral arrangements. Especially in the living room, where a gorgeous display of roses, baby's breath, spider mums and other flowers cascaded across the fireplace mantel. She knew that a bouquet for herself and a boutonniere for Deny were hidden in Maggie's car trunk. But she hadn't expected this. She made a mental note to thank Maggie for the lovely touch as she managed to detach herself and find a bathroom. She dabbed at her face and temples with a cold, wet washcloth and took deep breaths to calm her churning stomach.

At three o'clock a taxi stopped in front of the house and Deny got out. He was immediately engulfed by the mob of siblings and nieces and nephews who swarmed out the door to greet him. Elizabeth and her parents stayed inside, and she watched from the living room window and wondered if it was too late to bolt.

Obviously it was. Since she'd involved Maggie in this scenario of hers, she had no choice but to go through with it even if it killed her, and she was beginning to think that it very well might.

Elizabeth heard the surprise in Deny's voice as he greeted her dad and mom in the entryway. "Uncle Connor! Aunt Kathleen! I didn't know...I mean it's great to see you again."

Although she couldn't see them, Elizabeth knew they were locked in a three-way embrace while her mother cried softly and her dad cleared his throat. Deny didn't know *she* was here, either, and her stomach clenched as she waited for him to discover her.

After a few minutes that seemed like forever, the group in the entry started moving into the living room. Deny appeared with one arm around Maggie and the other around Kathleen. He was laughing and talking, and at first he didn't see Elizabeth.

She moved deeper into the shadow of the heavy drape, hoping for a few minutes to compose herself, but the magnetic attraction she felt must have pulled at him, too, because he looked up and directly at her.

She saw the blood drain from his face as he stared at her through eyes suddenly dulled with pain. She wanted to run to him, throw herself into his arms and beg him to forgive her for hurting him so badly, but she was almost certain that he wouldn't welcome such a display.

Instead, she managed to speak first. "Hello, Deny."

Deny felt as if he'd had the wind knocked out of him, and for a moment he could neither talk nor think straight. What was going on? No one had told him that Elizabeth and her parents would be having Thanksgiving dinner with them.

He couldn't keep his gaze from roaming over her. She was so breathtakingly beautiful in that beige lace dress. It had a high neck and long sleeves, almost like a bridal gown, but her soft, rounded curves underneath couldn't be camouflaged.

What was she doing here? Dammit, did she enjoy twisting the knife in his heart? Was she really that bent on vengeance?

He finally managed to gather his wits about him and respond. "Hello, Elizabeth."

Talk about scintillating conversation! They sounded like tongue-tied teenagers.

He finally managed to tear his gaze away from hers, and for several minutes he was inundated with questions and comments from the group surrounding him. They were eager to hear about the latest events in his life and to tell him about theirs.

When it began to look as if he were going to ignore her altogether, Elizabeth screwed up her courage and forced herself to walk across the room. She edged her way through the crowd of relatives surrounding him and when she was close enough, she reached out and put her hand on his arm.

He was wearing a navy blue suit, and she felt the muscles beneath her palm jump even through the fine wool of his coat sleeve.

For a few seconds she dared to hope that he wasn't as unaffected by her presence as he seemed, but then he turned his head to look down at her and his expression was cool, detached, with a touch of irritation at the intrusion.

Her stomach muscles knotted painfully, and she worried her lower lip with her teeth. He just stood there, silent and aloof, waiting for her to explain why she had interrupted.

Okay, so he wasn't going to make it easy for her. There was no reason why he should. He'd already done all he could to make things right between them. Now it was up to her.

Her fingers tightened on his arm, and she swallowed back the bile that rose in her throat. "Deny, I'm sorry to butt in like this, but it's really important that I talk to you. Will you please go up to your mom and dad's sitting room with me so we can have a little privacy?"

He looked startled. "Mom and dad's sitting room?"

She felt the hot flush that suffused her face. "It...it's the only place not filled with people. Except for the bedrooms..." Again her face flamed. "I...I mean—"

"I know what you mean, Elizabeth." His voice was almost as harsh as his expression. "However, I think we've said all that needs to be said to each other. There's nothing to be gained by reopening old wounds."

The house was thronged with people, and Elizabeth and Deny were standing right in the middle of the traffic. She had to talk to him and there was no way she could do it here.

"Please, Deny!" She heard the desperation in her tone but she couldn't help it. "What I have to say may not mean anything to you, but it's vitally important to me. Won't you give me just one more chance?"

He tensed, and his cool demeanor turned icy. "One more chance to what, Elizabeth? To tell me again what a rotten excuse for a human being I am? You've already made your point."

In her desperate need to make him stop talking and listen to her she said the first words that came into her mind. "Deny, do you still want to marry me?"

Her question had the desired effect. His jaw dropped, and his icy gaze turned to astonishment. Without another word he took her elbow and ushered her over to the staircase, up the stairs and into the east wing where his parents' quarters were located.

Elizabeth wasn't sure what he had in mind. Her question got him upstairs fast enough, but he sure wasn't hurrying to reassure her of his desire to make her his wife.

When they entered the sitting room, he closed and locked the door behind them, then turned to look at her. "All right," he said sternly. "Now talk."

The proposal of marriage was supposed to have come much later in her carefully prepared conversation with Deny, but now that she'd asked it, she was bound to go on from there.

She lifted her chin and held his gaze. "I asked you if you still want to marry me?"

His eyes never wavered. "No."

She gasped, and her own eyes widened with dismay. She'd thought she was prepared for a rejection, but she wasn't. Nowhere near. The single word *no* was like a jab to the stomach, and a swooshy "Ohhh" was torn from her throat as her knees gave way and she sank down onto the nearest chair.

Deny stood in front of her without moving, and his voice was laced with anger. "Stop playing games, Elizabeth. I want to know what in hell you're getting at. Last time I saw you you told me you'd never marry, and most especially you'd never marry me. So what's this all about? Didn't I grovel enough before? Or has your gentler nature taken over and you've decided to take pity on me and marry me to put me out of my misery?

"Well, forget it. I'm not going to be either your whipping boy or a sacrificial lamb to your conscience."

During the past week, Elizabeth had memorized everything she wanted to say to him. She'd polished the words and the tone inflections, then rehearsed them until she had them exactly right. Only Deny wasn't cooperating. He was giving all the wrong responses and had her so rattled that everything was driven from her mind except his short, succinct renunciation. *No!*

She took a deep breath and looked at him again. "*Are* you in misery, Deny?" Her voice was low but firm.

His mouth opened but he said nothing. When he finally spoke, it was again one sharp word. "Yes."

His admission should have reassured her, but it didn't. He obviously didn't want her sympathy.

Well, she'd found that wounded pride was a very cold and uncompromising companion. One she wouldn't hesitate to fling aside in an effort to change Deny's mind.

She glanced away, embarrassed but determined. "Then maybe you can understand how I feel," she said softly. "Is there any chance that you might marry me to put me out of *my* misery?"

She heard his shocked gasp, but when she looked up, his expression was still forbidding. "Why are you miserable, Elizabeth?" His voice wavered slightly.

She couldn't bear to sit there while he stood looking down on her. If she was going to plead with him, she was at least going to do it standing up.

She rose and turned away from him. "Because I know now that I threw away any chance I had for happiness when I refused to marry you."

"So you've changed your mind?"

She nodded, temporarily unable to speak.

His hands clutched her upper arms, gently but firmly. "Turn around and look at me when you talk to me," he commanded softly.

She obeyed, but he didn't release her. Instead his fingers massaged her shoulders, and his eyes were no longer cold. "I haven't heard the word *love* mentioned at all in this conversation. Do you love me?"

She blinked, unable to believe that he'd have to ask. "I've loved you for as far back as I can remember. Even when I thought I disliked you I knew I was fooling myself. The love was always there just under the surface, waiting for me to give myself permission to acknowledge it."

His expression softened slightly. "And what about trust? You said you could never marry me because you could never trust me again."

She couldn't resist reaching out to brush an errant lock of ebony hair off his forehead. "I trust you with my life and my happiness. Is that enough for you?"

Slowly he slid his hands from her shoulders, up her neck, to cradle either side of her head. "Not quite." His tone was low and rough with emotion. "You've forgotten a very important question. You haven't asked me if I love you."

She licked her dry lips. "I didn't forget. I'm afraid."

A flash of surprise twisted his features. "What are you afraid of, sweetheart?" It was almost a whisper.

She clung to the sound of that endearment, but, precious though it was to her, she couldn't rely on it meaning anything. He'd been calling her "sweetheart" for years. It probably just slipped out.

"I'm afraid you'll say no."

A ragged groan escaped from deep in Deny's chest as he lifted her upturned face and brushed his lips across hers, then again, and yet again before capturing her trembling mouth with his own in a kiss that combined the tenderness of innocence with the burgeoning desire of passion.

"I could never tell such a monstrous lie as that," he murmured as he settled her head on his shoulder and cuddled her against him. "I'd spend all of eternity in purgatory. I've loved you ever since I was three years old and your mother put you in my arms the day they brought you home from the hospital."

He chuckled. "I remember I thought she was giving you to me, and I put up one hell of a fight when she tried to take you back."

He sobered and lowered his head to nuzzle the sensitive hollow of her throat. "I wasn't strong enough to keep you then, but nobody will ever take you from me again. When do you want to get married?"

Her arms were twined around his neck, and she placed a string of tiny kisses under his jaw. "Right now."

"Right now! Here?" He lifted his head to look at her, disbelief written all over his face. "We can't get married today, much as I'd like to. It takes time—"

She raised her head and smiled. "Everything's all taken care of. All we have to do is walk down the stairs together and take the vows in front of the fireplace."

Deny frowned, and Elizabeth's heart sank. "I think you'd better tell me what in hell you're talking about," he said grimly. "You seem to have forgotten to send me an invitation to my own wedding."

She gasped and bent forward as the old bugaboo, nausea, swept over her. "Oh, no! Darling, it's not like that at all!" She fought to keep from being sick. "There were no invitations. I'm sorry, I didn't realize how it might look to you! Oh..."

A wave of dizziness swept over her and she swayed and stumbled backward. Deny caught her and held her close. "Elizabeth, my God, don't faint. You're white as a ghost. What's the matter? How long have you been sick?" He looked thoroughly frightened.

She shook her head against his shoulder. "It's nothing, really, I just...remember, I told you that I couldn't get married even if I wanted to because weddings make me physically ill?"

"That's right you did, but..." He rubbed his palm gently over her back. "You mean just the thought of marrying me does this to you?"

She raised her head to look at him. "Not just of marrying you. It's the thought of a wedding to anybody that does it. That's why I didn't discuss it with you first. I couldn't. I couldn't tell anyone, only Aunt Maggie and then only because I needed her help."

"My mother!"

Elizabeth nodded. "Yes, and she enlisted the aid of her lawyer and Father Murphy. No one else knows that Maggie and I were planning a wedding. If you hadn't wanted me, no one would ever have known about our plans, not even you."

Deny sagged against Elizabeth as if the series of shocks he'd been subjected to in the past hour had knocked the props out from under him. "Just let me get a couple of things straight," he said. "Is Father Murphy here? I didn't see him."

She smiled. "I'm sure he is by now. He was invited to dinner long before he was told that he may be asked to conduct a wedding before he gets fed."

"And the marriage license?" There was a note of anxiety in his tone. "How did you arrange—"

She raised her head and kissed him, effectively shutting off the rest of his sentence. "Don't ask," she murmured teasingly. "Aunt Maggie and her lawyer took care of that. All I know is you have to sign it in front of witnesses."

His arms tightened around her as he kissed her closed eyelids and her nose before taking her mouth and thoroughly exploring it. "Did you also make arrangements for a honeymoon?" he whispered huskily.

"Well," she drawled. "We'll have dinner right after the ceremony, and then I thought we could all sit around and watch football on television before breaking for a rousing game of charades. With such a large family, that should keep us busy for—"

"Elizabeth!" It was a cross between a growl and a groan, and she chuckled as she slowly and deliberately moved enticingly against him and nibbled on his lower lip.

"You don't like my plans?" she asked in her most seductive tone. "Well, fortunately I have an alternative. I reserved the honeymoon suite at the Four Seasons Clift Hotel for tonight. After that it's up to you."

He bit her earlobe gently, then whispered something that made her blush. "In that case," he said aloud, "we'd better get this show on the road. What I have in mind is going to take a long, long time."

"Oh, I hope so," she said with a sigh, and whispered something equally erotic in his ear.

*   *   *   *   *

If you've been looking for something a little bit different and a little bit spooky, let Silhouette Books take you on a journey to the dark side of love with

SILHOUETTE® Shadows™

Every month, Silhouette will bring you two romantic, spine-tingling Shadows novels, written by some of your favorite authors, such as *New York Times* bestselling author Heather Graham Pozzessere, Anne Stuart, Helen R. Myers and Rachel Lee—to name just a few.

In July, look for:
HEART OF THE BEAST by Carla Cassidy
DARK ENCHANTMENT by Jane Toombs

In August, look for:
A SILENCE OF DREAMS by Barbara Faith
THE SEVENTH NIGHT by Amanda Stevens

In September, look for:
FOOTSTEPS IN THE NIGHT by Lee Karr
WHAT WAITS BELOW by Jane Toombs

*Come into the world of Shadows and prepare
to tremble with fear—and passion....*

SHAD3

Is your father a Fabulous Father?

Then enter him in Silhouette Romance's

"FATHER OF THE YEAR" Contest
and you can both win some great prizes! Look for contest details in the FABULOUS FATHER titles available in June, July and August...

ONE MAN'S VOW by Diana Whitney
Available in June

ACCIDENTAL DAD by Anne Peters
Available in July

INSTANT FATHER by Lucy Gordon
Available in August

Only from

Silhouette
R O M A N C E™